A Drive to be Remembered

Book 1

of

Apocalypto

Aedan Sayla

(originally published under the pen name Frank Carlyle)

Aedan's books are available at: Amazon.com – Apple Books - Smashwords – Barnes & Noble – Kobo – Google Play Books – ebooks.com

Goodreads Page: Aedan Sayla

Author's Website: www.origins-of-love.org

Aedan Sayla's Blog – Musings: https://origins-of-love.org/musings

Author Contact Info: author-aedan-sayla@proton.me

A Drive to be Remembered / Aedan Sayla

Aedan Sayla

The Book List
(List last edited - 1/13/2023)

The Warriors of Mora Series
Book 1: *Submission of a Lady*
Book 2: *Warrioress Taming*
Book 3: *A Claimed Queen*
Book 4: *Possessing all of a Lady, Coming Soon*
Book 5: *The Unexpected Pleasure of a Slave, Coming Soon*

Apocalypto Series
Book 1: *A Drive to be Remembered*
Book 2: *Peril without Mercy*
Book 3: *The Will to Thrive, Coming Soon*

The Agents Series
Book 1: *Agent in Training*
Book 2: *Finding an Agent, Coming Soon*

Escaping Babylon Series
Book 1: *Foreign Princess, Coming Soon*
Book 2: *Queen in Hiding, Coming Soon*

The Badlands Series
Book 1: *The Baron Killer, Coming Soon*
Book 2: *The Cold Killers, Coming Soon*

American Apocalypse Series
Book 1: *City - Prison Land, Coming Soon*
Book 2: *Forest - Freedom Land, Coming Soon*

Standalone Books

Book: *The Huntsman*
Book: *Man on Fire*
Book: *A Russian Rose*
Book: *Tomorrow's Woman*
Book: *A Lady's Worth*
Book: *Charity's Gunman*
Book: *A Rebel's Persuasion*
Book: *Book Mate*
Book: *Brides of War*
Book: *Broken but Undefeated*
Book: *Cave Man*
Book: *Surrender's Passion*
Book: *The Forbidden Zone*
Book: *The Slave Princess, Coming Soon*
Book: *Lost, Coming Soon*
Book: *The Last Incan, Coming Soon*
Book: *His - Beauty in the Dark, Coming Soon*

Content Warning

Dear reader, if per chance you did not see otherwise – this is a work of erotic fiction. The erotic content is quite vividly portrayed.

All primary sexual relations that take place are of a heterosexual standard and the age of the characters involved is 18+.

There are several scenes of both apocalyptic and sexual violence including a scene of almost forced non-consent.

The appropriate reading age is 18+.

Original Ancient Erotica from the Bible

"1 Behold, thou art fair, my love; behold, thou art fair; thou hast doves' eyes within thy locks: thy hair is as a flock of goats, that appear from mount Gilead.

2 Thy teeth are like a flock of sheep that are even shorn, which came up from the washing; whereof every one bear twins, and none is barren among them.

3 Thy lips are like a thread of scarlet, and thy speech is comely: thy temples are like a piece of a pomegranate within thy locks.

4 Thy neck is like the tower of David builded for an armoury, whereon there hang a thousand bucklers, all shields of mighty men.

5 Thy two breasts are like two young roes that are twins, which feed among the lilies.

6 Until the day break, and the shadows flee away, I will get me to the mountain of myrrh, and to the hill of frankincense.

7 Thou art all fair, my love; there is no spot in thee."

Song of Solomon 4:1-7 KJV

CONTENTS

Stalked

Raising the bullhorn to my lips I called out through it as the surf washed around my ankles, "That's far enough. You two over by the rocks you need to get back in and closer to the shore. There are dangerous undertows over there."

The two tourists I had directed my amplified voice at reacted with the typical surprise of someone being called out and quickly made away from the rocks.

"Thank you." I called out with satisfaction through the bullhorn. Letting the bullhorn fall down to brush against my thigh I ambled back along the beach to my lifeguard station.

My summer job, as a lifeguard, wasn't all that overly rewarding except for one thing. I got to be in a continuous relationship with the ocean.

Ever since growing up as a girl in Cape Town, South Africa to now studying to be an oceanographer at a university exchange program here in Oregon I had loved anything to do with the water. My parents said that I had spent more time in the water than out of it and they might just be right on that one.

I climbed up the steps to my lofty seat cast in shade by an umbrella and commenced to oversee the domain of Oregon beachfront that I was responsible for. Summer vacation had started a month back and I had wanted to go back to South Africa to visit, but one of the professors had asked for my help on a research project and so I had stayed behind.

Right now though I wish I hadn't. So much was going strangely these days and I had the innate desire to be with my friends and family as opposed to being by myself on these foreign shores of America.

I had friends here, but to them I was just the slightly odd South African Christian girl with a funny accent. If it wasn't my accent it seemed to be something about my refusal to join the party lifestyles of my fellow classmates that seemed to set me apart from the status quo of the current liberal times here in America.

I wasn't changing; however, just to suit them, but I did feel very much alone and once more I regretted my decision to stay here for the summer.

Speaking of being alone - he was back.

I leaned forward on my perch to study the silent individual who sat about a hundred feet further up the beach in his usual spot.

This man was a complete enigma to me.

He was always alone. I never saw him arrive, but suddenly he would be there sitting on the beach, staring out at the crashing waves as if wanting to be a part of the action, but apart from it as if bound by some invisible hand.

He never went into the water, but he stared at it for hours. It was the only thing that kept his attention, except for one other thing - me.

He stared at me.

The way he stared at me was alarming, because I knew what he was thinking. He wanted me sexually and he did nothing to hide it, but gazed at me with a frank forthrightness that had caused me to come to silently fear just the sight of him.

He was big in a way that was more than just being tall and muscular. He had an ingrained intensity and discipline about him that said he had the ability to seize a giant twice his size and break him in half over his knee.

The degree of coldness about him was perhaps the most off-putting of all. He seemed devoid of emotion other than the urge I saw within him to be swimming in the ocean and to sexually be having at me.

It had gotten to the point that I hated to even walk past him, because of the way his eyes seemed to stalk after me. I did not feel safe around him at all.

Truly many men, mostly tourists, openly lusted for me in the course of my duties as I made my rounds along the beach. It was unavoidable as it seemed that most men anymore didn't seem to have any manners and in general it was easy for me to pray for them and just move on and disregard their open lust for me, as well as their called out whistles and comments engineered to spark further communication, as if I existed as some sexy playmate for their desires simply because I was a lifeguard and too many of them had grown up watching Baywatch.

Even as I disregarded them I couldn't do the same for him. I felt threatened by him and it was with relief that he was always gone from the beach before my shift was over and I had to make my way to the often vacant parking lot where I had to then wait for a taxi to pick me up.

There were no lights or security cameras and it was an unpleasant thing, as a young, attractive woman, to have to wait for the taxi to come. I'd asked to have the early shift, but my request had been declined and so I was tasked with closing the beach in the evening.

Really, I should just quit and tell my professor good luck and go home until school started up again. The more I thought about it as I gazed at the man, who had become my silent nemesis, I realized the validity of what a good idea that was.

Getting a couple of extra credits was not worth getting mugged, putting up with tourists, or of being stalked by a man that scared me.

It was with surprise then that I realized something in regards to my uncomfortable feelings engineered by this man.

With all the worry and angst he had put me through I had failed to do the one thing that I should've done first. I hadn't taken it to God in prayer.

Wasting no time I closed my eyes and prayed, "Dear God, I need Your help. This man scares me and I'm not supposed to give into fear, but I have and now I'm giving You my fears. Please help me and keep me safe and show me whether I should quit and go home or not. Also, the man, even though I feel that he is my enemy.... he seems to be broken in some way. I don't know what he is struggling with, but I pray that You would help him and make a way by which he can become whole, and if he doesn't already have a relationship with Your Son, Jesus, then I pray that he would soon find it. In Jesus's Name, I ask and pray these things."

I opened my eyes and looked around. Everything was the same, but I felt emboldened.

It was time to make my rounds and I climbed down and began to make my way up the beach. Almost as if he had the benefit of sonar to aid him I witnessed my silent watcher turn his head from the ocean to view me.

His look of forlorn wistfulness that he had been giving the ocean now turned into one of open hunger as his eyes ran over me possessively. Perhaps that was why his lust for me bothered me so much.

Other men lusted for me, but his look said that I belonged to him, as if it was some foregone conclusion and that I had no choice in the matter. My old fears rose up sharply within me and I was on the verge of passing him by when I turned instead to approach him.

His gaze took in my advance upon him with nothing but lustful interest, where other men having been caught might have looked away and acted as if they hadn't been looking at me. Not him though.

Coming to a stop in the hot sand I spoke out my thoughts, as best as I could state them, all the while feeling like a defenseless bunny in front of a devouring wolf, "Sir, I know this is a free country and so as you have broken no law there is nothing I can do to change a situation that I do not like. I do not like the way you look at me, but as a person with a God-given choice you have the right to look at me; however you wish to, but I humbly ask that you would not look at me as you do. I'm sorry if my skimpy attire is a distraction for you, but it's sadly dress code for this profession. Perhaps what would be best is for you to pick a different section of the beach for you to sit upon. If that's not doable then I'm going to need to resign my position here and…and……." Sounding utterly ridiculous to even my own ears, I threw my hands up and stalked away down the beach and just like always I felt his lusting gaze follow after me.

Words could not describe how much of an idiot I felt like in the moment. Thankfully, no one else had been close enough to hear my truly entitled sounding rant.

I was not an entitled minded person though. I was simply scared and I had no one to be a source of security for me in a difficult situation.

There was just no other way of getting around it - I needed to quit my job and go home.

I nodded my head to that resolution as my blonde hair whipped about my face on a sudden landward breeze.

With the breeze came a spoken word into my soul that had me come to a standstill in the sand, **"Jolana?"**

Shaking inwardly and probably outwardly I whispered in reply, "Yes, God?"

"It's too late to go home. Judgment upon this nation and the beginning of sorrows for many other nations within the world has begun, but you are set apart to Me and I've made a way by which your life will be spared, if you so wish it to be so."

Feeling tears streak down my face I asked in shock, "I can't go home?"

"Your home is in Me. I will keep you. Be patient child and you will see."

Nothing more came to me and wiping at my face I gazed around at the happy vacationers enjoying themselves in the sand and surf as if they didn't have a care in the world. I on the other hand felt like screaming at the top of my lungs in hopes of waking them up to what I had just been alerted of in the spirit to by my God.

Suddenly there was screaming and with alarm I looked up and out to sea. A surfer far out past the main traffic on the beach was floundering about and crying out unintelligibly.

With renewed focus I sprang into action as my training took over.

I raced back to my station and grabbed the preserver board and tied it off before then running down the beach and plunging into the surf. I was a powerful swimmer, but he was far out and by the time I neared him I was out of breath and taxed physically.

The situation I faced though immediately sent chills down my spine as instead of a cramped up wakeboarder I was presented with a man missing half his arm. Blood was gushing everywhere and the man was beside himself with terror.

Careful to avoid his attempts to latch hold of me and likely drown us both I pulled the preserver board close to me and began to extend it outward to him when something huge brushed by me. The water foamed white before me and broke apart, as if a wave had suddenly erupted.

The shark for that was what it was chomped into the preserver and ripped it from my hands before splitting through the water between me and the struggling man, who now screamed manically upon seeing the shark once more.

I screamed too, as I was abruptly pulled through the water and then beneath it.

In terror my eyes took in the fact that I was being pulled along by the shark because of the preserver's line wrapped around my ankle. Thankfully, the strap pulled off my ankle and I backpedaled away from the underwater monster with my effort to rise to the surface and escape from it.

In my one track thought of escaping one threat to my life I gave authorship to another, as my head came above the surface of the water and I bumped accidentally into the injured surfer.

Almost instantly my head was plunged back downward beneath the water as the surfer latched onto me.

I needed air, but the man was almost twice my size and aided by the adrenaline of fear in his effort to be free of the water he held me down. Struggling to rise up for air and break away from him I stopped in terror as my eyes took in the fast-moving object of toothed terror that was coming in fast at me from below!

Oh God, I was going to die!

None of what was happening this day made sense!

Despite my training and long exposure to being in the water I lost everything to fear and screamed, but despite my cloud of bubbles nothing happened and then it did.

Something slammed into the shark and blood gushed everywhere, as did the water, as the huge shark thrashed about mightily.

Unwittingly though the intense current of disturbed water forced me up to the surface and I gasped for air, only to be plunged back under by the surfer who now had a painful grip on my hair. I blinked, but the water was awash with blood and I couldn't see anything.

There was a struggle suddenly from beside me and the pressure keeping me under suddenly went slack. Something latched onto my arm and about pulled it out of its socket as it tugged me upward.

I crested the surface of the water and gasped for air, which is when I saw him. The man I'd told to stop watching me.

The man I had to now credit with saving my life somehow.

His voice loud, but dim sounding at the same time called out, "You alright?"

Not waiting for an answer, he reached out and slapped me none too gently on the face, but some part of me knew that I needed the pain to help refocus and my breathing picked up to normal again.

I half choked out, "I'm okay."

Even as I acknowledged fuzzily that I was in shock and desperately needed to get out of the water.

As if opening my eyes for the first time I gazed about. With a little scream, I shot away from the sight of something massive and bloody nearby.

"Relax, baby girl, its dead." Came the terse response from my nemesis of the past month.

Foggily my mind took in the fact that this man had somehow killed a shark. I had been right about him, he was as dangerous as I'd thought he was and more and yet he'd risked his life to save mine.

"Hey, Princess, you mind giving me a hand here?"

Dazedly, I spun in the water to behold my nemesis struggling to keep the unconscious surfer's head above the water, as he tried to twist off a tourniquet about the man's upper arm at the same time.

Training helped me spring into action and moving forward I stabilized the man in the water so that he could focus on tying the man's arm off.

Tying it off, he took hold of the man once more and giving me a cursory look he asked, "What's your name, Princess?"

"Jolana." I replied dazedly.

"Well, Jolana, we need to get to shore now. Can you swim?"

Nodding, I turned about in the water, but my sense of direction didn't seem to be working. His big hand grasped a hold of the back of my neck and he moved me around in the water in a new direction even as he dryly commented, "This way, Princess."

Still dazed, I asked, "Why are you calling me that?"

His hand was gone from my neck and then I gasped with surprise as I felt it sharply smack across my bottom. I surged forward in the water away from him only to hear his words drift along after me, "Because you act like one."

I began swimming then and I didn't stop until my toes dug into the sand of the beach. Forcing myself to stop I turned to help the man bring the surfer up out of the waves and onto the beach where miraculously an ambulance was already parked with all its lights glistening.

The surfer was taken from us and very much feeling like I was functioning on autopilot, I stumbled off to my station. Clumsily claiming a hold of my bullhorn I pulled it up to announce, "The beach is closed. Please leave. I'm sorry, but the beach is closed."

There really had been no need for the words as tourists everywhere were flocking to their cars and getting the heck out of Dodge.

Glancing around at the pandemonium I idly watched as the carcass of what I identified as an adult great white shark came floating bloodily in to be stranded on the sands of the beach. How on earth was such a thing possible?

I should be dead, but I wasn't just as God had told me that I would be preserved, even so I had been from certain death. And of all means of accomplishing it, God had used my nemesis of all people to do it!

I sat down upon the sand abruptly.

Nothing made sense!

Pulling my knees up to my chest I pressed my face against them as I realized for the first time how badly I was shivering. A warm towel was draped around my back and shoulders, followed by a second one across the front of my legs and my feet.

Glancing up I saw it was him again and whispering out softly I said, "Thank you."

He grunted and looked away for a moment before taking his soaked T-shirt off. My gaze took in the resplendently ripped physique of not only an athlete, but one who was a warrior as well.

He was beautiful to behold and yet I could see scars, and even what I took to be healed over bullet holes. He did nothing but stand there bare chested gazing out at the ocean once more.

Forcing my eyes to leave him I glanced elsewhere, only to take in the fact that the beach was entirely deserted of every last living soul that had just populated it but minutes before.

Oh God, I was here alone with him!

I flinched slightly as he abruptly sat down on the sand beside me.

Sighing, he asked out loud while still gazing out at the ocean, "Why are you so afraid of me?"

There it was - an honest question.

Honesty deserved an answer and my lips feeling numb, I tried to give life to one, "Because of the way you look at me. You make me feel like I'm a prey animal and that you're the tiger waiting to spring and sink its fangs into the back of my neck."

He nodded his head and then giving a bittersweet smile he said, "True enough, I guess, only it wouldn't be my teeth that I'd sink into you."

He glanced at me and not wanting to play any games with this man, I asked "Are you going to rape me?"

"Do you want me to?"

"No." I whispered back in reply.

He glanced back out to sea and so did I. I didn't know what was going to happen, but I wasn't going to leave unsaid what needed to be said, "Thank you for saving my life. Whatever you decide to do, I thank you for what you did earlier."

It was said now and with unsteady lips I continued staring out to sea, as he turned his head to look at me.

Glancing away, he rubbed at his face for a moment before saying, "Actually, I have something I need to thank you for."

I glanced at him in surprise and asked, "What?"

"You got me back into the water. I....... it's been a while and I thought I was all washed up, but....... maybe I'm not. I killed a shark today." He said the last as if it was a reassuring clue of perceived manliness.

What on earth could make this man lack in the confidence of his own masculinity?

He practically exuded raw maleness. A maleness that ached to possess my body and it wasn't just because I was pretty.

In my study of him this past month I'd noticed him not pay attention to any woman the way that he had to me. Why was that?

The Spirit of my Creator softly commented into my thoughts, **"He's lost and like a moth in the dark he's attracted to the brightness of your soul, Jolana."**

Feeling as if my breath had been taken from me, I silently asked God, *"How far do You intend for this to go? I mean…… what…… I don't understand this."*

"I know. Child, look up."

I did and when I did I gasped out loud as my eyes took in the sight of a huge fireball that seemed to take up half the sky with its brilliance as it streaked out overhead in the direction of the ocean. The man beside me saw it and cursing in exclamation he stood up, while I stayed where I was in shock.

"Everything is about to change child. How far you wish to go I leave for you to decide. Stay here on the beach and soon I will gather you along with your family into My everlasting Kingdom, as one of my favored children, or leave now with him and I will safeguard you in the difficulties of life ahead and bring forth good fruit of your union with him."

Feeling tears streak down my face I breathed out in brokenness, "My family?"

"With Me already, child. They will know no more pain, only My joy for all of eternity."

Breathing out I said, "This is why I stayed this summer, isn't it? You wanted me here in America. Why?"

I glanced up to the man that stood as if spell locked, as he gazed out over the ocean at the fiery ball of color that was sinking ever lower towards the waves.

"If I stay here on the beach he dies." I said softly, as if acknowledging what had already becoming a fact somehow.

"Yes, he will and he will be forever separated from Me for all of eternity."

My hand rose up to my mouth as the awful reality of what hell would be like became a full reality to me as I gazed upon this man, who would soon be there if I did not act. I did not like him at all or care for him, but I wished for no man what I knew to be a future without hope cast off into endless torment.

"You want me to go with him?" I silently queried seeking the support I needed of my Creator's, Holy Spirit to make a choice that I never would have believed would've been asked of me.

"It's your choice, Jolana."

I stood up feeling shaken to the core of my being and still reeling with the emotion that I would never see my family again.

I tugged on the man's arm and dazedly he glanced at me and feeling stripped raw to the depths of my spirit, I said, "Do you believe in hell?"

I didn't wait for him to answer before I continued on with intensity, "Well, I do and I tell you right now that you're headed straight there if we don't leave this beach right now!"

Again, I didn't wait for a response, but grabbing a hold of his hand, I tugged him up the beach towards the parking lot and the only vehicle left in it, his Jeep. Reaching it, I let go of his hand and went around it to the passenger door.

I'd expected him to go to his side, but he was behind me and then opening the door before me. Feeling very weird still dressed in only a bikini I climbed up to sit down into the passenger seat of the Jeep.

Oh, why hadn't I grabbed my clothes or at least a towel!

But then what did it matter anyway.

He was taking longer than expected and I started to turn to look for him, when out of breath, he appeared at the driver door of the Jeep. He jumped in and tossed of all things my clothes and purse at me.

He'd even brought my shoes!

Stunned, I looked down at them laying on my lap, as he brought the Jeep alive and cranked it into reverse and then forward as he peeled out of the parking lot.

Dazedly, I pulled my tank top over my bikini and then precariously pulled on my Capri pants as he drove like a crazy man. Capri pants on I hastily buckled my seatbelt and wiped at the tears on my face that had never seemed to stop.

Like it or not I had made a big decision in what I had chosen to do and I knew what it would surely lead to in regards to him, but it had been nice of him to get my clothes and shoes like he had done. It was nice to know that he could be nice.

It helped somehow knowing that he was capable of that.

I glanced over at him to see sweat rolling down his face.

Feeling very calm I reached over and laid my hand on his knee.

He glanced at me and to my surprise, I saw fear; great fear. Not of me, but of something else.

Soothingly I said, "Relax, you're going to be okay, but if possible I think you need to drive even faster."

His eyes traced from me to the speedometer that was already pegged at over a 100mph. Not saying anything though I saw him stomp harder on the gas and I did my best then to hold onto the contents of my stomach as we peeled around curves and stopped motorists gazing off after the trail of the asteroid - like bugs zoned into the bright glow of a bugzapper in the gloom of the night.

"Where should I go?" He gritted out, as he dodged around a slow-moving minivan.

"Inland as fast as you can go. You need to get to high ground, preferably past Interstate 5."

His jaw moved powerfully and he pressed on the gas even more. At that moment the road heaved beneath us and if it hadn't been for my seatbelt I would've banged my head off of the ceiling.

How he kept the Jeep upright as we spun one way and then the other I do not know, other than that I could never hope to equal such driving skills. He cursed and I saw the road up ahead was blocked by two vehicles.

We were too close to stop at the speed we were going at and yet God had promised and armed me with a hope and so amazingly un-concerned I said, "I'd really appreciate it if you'd stop cursing like that. Taking the Lord's name in vain is not a good thing to do."

He spared one disbelieving look at me before redirecting focus and slamming the Jeep into neutral before then spinning the wheel hard. The jeep skidded around until its rear outraced the front, but in doing such the jeep skidded in a trajectory that curveballed through the nar-row gap between the vehicles and coming to a sliding stop in the dust off to the side of the road he jammed it back into drive and with heavy treaded tires ripping and spewing sand and gravel we took off again forward with the velocity of a rocket taking off.

Feeling glued to my seat and seeing double I wasn't expecting it when he said, "I'll get right to work on that, Princess."

I glanced at him. His tone hadn't been as overly sarcastic as it had been bemused sounding.

Curiously, I asked, "What's your name?"

"Orrin."

"Mine is, Jolana." I stated intentionally reminding him of the fact that he already knew my name.

"As you wish, Princess." He replied back with equal intentionality.

I don't know why, but I smiled at his response, as we swerved about fallen rocks in the road and other vehicles with such seemingly superlative ease that I couldn't refrain from asking, "Exactly what is it that you do for a living?"

"I was a Navy Seal once and then other things, but I got washed up."

I glanced at him to see the bitterness that I'd heard in his words fully mar across his unmistakably very handsome face.

Feeling around for something to say to soften the tightness that my question had brought to him I said, "You killed a shark today."

The tension in his shoulders eased slightly and then glancing at me he accusingly asked, "Why are you being nice to me all of a sudden?"

It was a hard question to answer, but finding one I tugged at my shirt hem and said, "You were nice to me."

"Just being practical."

"How's that?" I asked.

"You're distracting enough without having you permanently so."

I stared at him in surprise and then curiously I asked, "I'm not distracting you now?"

He started to curse, but he stopped mid-note.

Looking over at me he aggressively said, "Why don't you just shut up!"

He returned his glance to the road ahead, as he gripped the wheel hard, before then glancing in his rearview mirror.

It was clear that he was trying to ignore me, but not put off I asked, "Are you worried about dying?"

"Aren't you?" He accused harshly.

"No." I replied back with honesty.

He glanced at me uncertainly and I met his gaze for a moment before gazing away to the road ahead. We'd reached a main road and our speed was once more well over a 100mph.

I didn't quite know how to put what needed to be said, but I tried, "I made a big decision back there on the beach to come with you. I don't know if you've fully realized it yet or not, but life is never going to be the same. Society, everything is going to change and it's going to be a fight just to survive. For someone with your background that won't be such a problem, but you're not alone anymore. You have a woman to think of. Can you promise me that you're going to do your best to look out for me and save me, if need be, from tough situations and the abuse of others that would wish to harm me? If you can't promise that then you need to stop right now and let me out, because I'm not going another mile with you, if you're not capable or willing to be a caretaker of me."

Wiping at the trails of sweat rolling off his forehead Orrin gave me a speculative glance that said he was very unsure as to what to think of me.

Stating his thoughts plainly, which was something I really liked about him, he said, "You know you're really weird!"

"Answer the question, Orrin. I'm serious."

He glanced at me and for emphasis I put my hand on the doorknob. He glanced from it and then to me as with a ready intelligence he surmised the situation up by saying, "You'd really jump out wouldn't you."

Woodenly I said, "I've got nothing left to live for. My family, the people I care about most, are all dead. It would be very easy to go and join them right now."

Fresh tears streaked down my face as the full memory of my loss hit home once more.

"How do you know they're dead?" Orrin asked softly.

"God told me." I responded with upfrontly before pressing hard with, "Well how about it? Are you in or out, because soon I'm out!"

My hand pulled on the handle and crying out he said, "Wait! I……. what are we even talking about here? I mean…… I………?"

"It's simple, Orrin. The question is are you going to be responsible for me and care for me as a man would for his mate?"

"Why would you want me to be that?" He asked expressing genuine surprise.

I shook my head, "I don't, but I want……. I want you to have a chance. I'm willing to be used to that end to give you a chance at heaven, but I'm not making such a sacrifice for any no account stalking deadbeat that doesn't have the guts to speak up for what he wants!"

I'd said the words plainly and his response was quick and sincere, as he dodged his gaze away from the hazards of the road to me to say, "I want you and I'll do whatever it takes to keep you safe! Please don't jump!"

A calm peace settled over me then and I willingly allowed it to change me. I settled back into my seat and took my hand off the doorknob.

I heard him release a pent up breath and then he asked, "What……. why do you even trust what I say?"

"I don't know." I answered truthfully.

I glanced at him and then stated, "I've given myself to you, but if you go back on your promise heaven help you! Now if you wish to live to claim your reward I suggest that you start driving faster."

He glanced at me with a look of both confusion and the intense passion he had for me. I pointed to the rearview mirror and he glanced at it only to then curse viciously at the sight of a towering wave in the far-off distance.

"Don't curse." I said, but my words were lost in the roar of the Jeep as he taxed it for all it was worth.

I turned my head away and gazed idly at the wave approaching from the rear.

Silently, I prayed, *"I've done my part. I'll try my best, but I need Your help. I don't like this road You have me on at all!"*

"I know, child." Came my answering response and I closed my eyes, as fresh tears welled up and spilled out from my eyes, as no deliverance from the future that I had agreed upon came to greet me by way of a reprieve.

CHAPTER TWO

Overwhelmed

"You're a Christian, right?" Orrin suddenly commented tensely from the driver's seat interrupting my misery filled forecast of what the future would be like.

I turned my head to him and asked, "How did you know that?"

"It shows." was all he said, before admitting, "I'm not ready to die, but I'm going to in short order if something doesn't change!"

Seeing a new aspect of this man that had been pressed to the limit I reached out a hand and patted his shoulder reassuringly to say, "You'll be all right. Take the next right that you come to."

"Why?" He asked uncertainly.

"Don't know, but something says that's what you should do."

He gave me a quick glance before then glancing once more at the rearview mirror. A junction lay just up ahead and curiously I waited to see what he would do.

He actually slowed down despite the surging tsunami of all waves behind us and on two wheels we rounded the corner and sped down the secondary road.

It led into a valley and abruptly the road hooked around a rise in the topography and with the tires screeching Orrin took the chance that he saw.

He sped up a gravel inclined pathway that led upward toward the top of a knoll that was now buffered between us and the oncoming wave.

"Stop." I said and instantly he did to the point that I was flung against my seatbelt and had the breath half knocked out of me.

Air wheezing back into my lungs I glanced at him as I saw him engage the parking brake.

Speaking out loud, I stated, "You actually trust me don't you."

His face was awash with sweat and nervous tension and tersely, he said, "You're the one that claims to be talking to God and all! I ain't got nothing!" He exclaimed out at the last.

I patted his knee, "You have me."

He glanced at me and then we both looked forward as the top of the immense wave shot out over the top of the knoll even as a power slide of water surged around the sides of the knoll and filled the valley behind us up almost to the brim.

Water cascaded down upon the Jeep and I feared that the windshield would cave in under the pressure of the endless water cresting out over the top of the knoll.

Why we weren't swept away, I did not know other than that the Jeep seemed to be completely rooted in place. My hand found Orrin's and together we held each other's hand tightly as an endless barrage of seawater swept down over us.

Tears came to my eyes again as the unimaginable loss of human life today made its full impact on me. So many had died, were dying and would die in the days to come.

The thought of how humanity would turn on itself in the aftermath of such a global disaster was a horror in and of its own. I glanced over to the man who would no doubt possess my body very soon and I wondered for the thousandth time if my choice to attempt to save his soul was truly worth the effort it would take just to survive him and what remained of the world in the aftermath of this disaster.

I didn't know, but I'd made the choice and now I had to live with it.

I closed my eyes as the endless deluge of water continued to wash over us and somehow in the midst of destruction I went to sleep.

~~~~~~

Startled, I sat up in my seat.

The water had stopped and Orrin was gone!

His door was open. Pulling my shoes on I got out and gasped aloud at what I saw.

The land was stripped bare and strewn with the carnage of debris gathered up of the remains of every seaside community along the coast of Oregon. The sky was a sooty gray and in the distance I could see magma shooting into the sky in a fiery display of molten heat.

The red glow of lava lent an eerie color over this ransacked countryside that would never be the same again. The Jeep was left alone of everything that had existed on top of the knoll.

That by itself was a miracle, but looking out at the devastation I could only wonder at how we could hope to survive in such a landscape as this.

Was farther inland any better than what I saw around me?

Large hands settled around my waist and I would've jumped away if they hadn't held me in place. Breathing a little heavier I leaned forward to get away, but Orrin's hold on me didn't budge.

I felt his head, then as he ducked it into the side of my neck and breathed in deeply the smell of my skin and hair.

"Orrin I...... please don't!" I said, as my hands pulled at his.

His voice sounding raw in my ear he said, "You have your faith in God to help you face the devastation of all you see, but I have nothing, except you!"

The emotion of his words touched me and I realized that it was true. I stopped pulling at his hands and when I did that he swept me up
~~~~~~

into his arms and in the glow of the far-off magma he carried me to the back end of the Jeep.

He set me down on my feet and I backed up several feet as he opened the back hatch and threw stuff to the side before half crawling in to slam the rear seats down flat.

He got back out and I beheld a man of emotional passion that looked at me as if I was the only bright spot left in the world.

He stood where he was and yet the intent within his eyes to seize a hold of me was there, but he didn't.

Feeling shaken to my core I stuttered out softly with, "What are you waiting for?"

"You!" He breathed out shakily.

I looked away and then back and took in all that he was. This was not at all how I'd wanted to be in life when I came to the stage of being a man's mate, but the circumstances were what they were.

Trembling, I stepped forward and his hands seized a hold of me. I was lifted and laid down into the Jeep in virtually the same second.

Breathing heavy I lay there and then he was there straddling above me completely naked, with a look in his eyes that was almost animal.

What had I done!

My fearing gaze swept down over his muscles and seized in horror upon the burgeoning proof of his manliness. I'd seen the pictures here and there of a man's cock in full arousal as it was hard not to on a promiscuous college campus, but nothing could prepare me for this!

He was huge and beyond anything I had ever expected to have to accommodate in my body and with a scream, I tried to push away to escape from the animal that this man had suddenly become. Truly, this was my worst nightmare come to life, only instead of the sands of the parking lot it was taking place in the back of his Jeep and this time there really was no one to come to my rescue.

"Oh God!" I cried out as I struggled to be free, but it was no good and in a heartbeat I found myself flipped onto my front. Pushing up to shuffle forward only succeeded in having my hands pulled out from beneath me and tied off behind my back.

My face pressed to the back of the flattened down seat I cried out, "Please stop!"

"We had a deal Princess or have you forgotten that?" He said savagely from behind me even as I felt his hands undo my capris.

He was right, but how could he be?

How had I ever agreed to this and yet I surely had.

Closing my eyes, I stopped fighting, as I felt my Capris ripped down my legs, until I was bare except for my bikini bottoms.

I heard him groan and pressing my face against the back of the seat I said, "Please untie me. I won't try to escape."

There was a long pause and then my hands were free and I brought them up to either side of my face, but I remained still.

Brokenly I said then, "What do you want me to do?"

"Get onto your knees." He said huskily and I did so all the while feeling the most vulnerable I ever had in my life.

The strings of my bikini bottom were undone by his fingers and I heard him groan with appreciation again and then his hands were on the cheeks of my bottom in a way that no man's hands ever had been before.

Whispering out I said, as he spread my knees apart and moved in between them, "Could you please put something on your...... your shaft to help you slide in. I...... please."

I really didn't expect for him to do anything, but I heard him rummaging into something and then I heard the sound of what I took to be his hand moving upon his shaft. Maybe it wouldn't be as painful now, but I had no real hope for that because he was absolutely huge and I wasn't all that big of a girl to accept a shaft like his, but somehow despite how tight I might be I knew he'd force every inch of himself into me.

I felt a heady thrill despite everything that was terrible about the moment and in shock I tried to do away with the thought of taking pleasure in anything that was about to happen as it just seemed wrong to do so. I felt his fingers split apart the lips of my womanhood and then the head of his shaft was nestled wetly into the intimate clasp of the lips of my vagina.

Shivering with nervous anticipation of all that was to come I felt his hands close warmly over my hips even as his belly came in full contact with my bottom. The world had just been destroyed and in a moment, so would my virginity to a man I would never have picked out as a mate, but was likely the best option I had for continued survival in a torn apart land such as existed now.

"Thank you, Princess, for not fighting this!" He breathed out as he began to press the aggressiveness of his passion into me far more slowly than I had expected him to.

What was giving him restraint in this moment when he seemed to be a man without any when it came to me?

I gasped continually as I felt the bulging girth of him make way into me, but then his shaft came to a resisting stop.

His grip on my hips was savage, even as his voice matched it for savagery as he said, "You're a virgin! God, what a monster I've become!"

To my shock then I felt him withdraw his shaft completely from me and move back to then jump off the back of the Jeep.

Raising up onto my hands, I looked behind me to see him standing with his hands on his hips, staring up at the ash filled skies as his shaft continued to stand out in full passioned arousal.

I started to move out of my position of submissiveness, but a voice from within said, **"No."**

Biting my lip I stayed on my knees. So be it then.

Calling out to him I said, "I agreed to be your woman, Orrin. You aren't wrong to claim me. I...... you can still claim me."

He looked away from the sky to me and his face reflected intense emotion and perhaps some kinder look than I had seen upon his face before. He came then toward me and the look of him was just so much raw power that I looked forward once more.

I didn't want to see just how big he was again.

The vehicle depressed under his weight and then with a gasp, I felt him warmly pressed up against me again. His hands massaged over my back, as I held still once more, as he made an entrance into my vagina that felt too tight to accommodate even half of him.

Breathing heavy I felt him come to a stop once more at the barrier within me and I couldn't help but tense at the expected pain of his penetration into me. He leaned down over my back with his hands clasped over my shoulders and said into my ear, "Thank you, Jolana."

The sound of my name from off of his lips was a kinder thing then I'd expected of him to say and it sent a thrill through me and then I gasped out loud as his one hand swept my blonde hair aside only for me to then feel his teeth bite down securely over the back of my neck.

Something wild was unleashed within me and then in a heartbeat all thought was gone as his shaft shattered through my virginity and pierced into the core of my being.

I cried out in pain and the desire to escape, but his hold on my neck and shoulders held me still as he grindingly shoved all of himself into me so much so that I felt as if he was coming up the back of my throat.

Overwhelmed and shaking, I wasn't able to handle any of what I felt let alone the feel of his massive shaft drawing back only to press forward again and stretch apart my inner depths for his complete possession of them.

His teeth left my neck and breathing unsteadily, he groaned out, "You are so unbelievably tight!"

His hand pressed gently on the back of my neck and I collapsed down onto my face as he straightened up fully and seized a hold of my hips in a way that promised to never let go. Everything changed then as he savagely stroked his shaft as deep as it would go into me again and again.

Panting, I pressed my face to the seat as I felt his seed begin to splash hotly within me in great volume.

I had never imagined being with a man would be like this!

Something was being stroked within me that felt both odd and wonderful and it was a feeling that I didn't want to let go to, but again there came that voice of the Highest within my soul, **"Let go, child."**

I did then, as if compelled to, and as Orrin thrust his throbbing seed spent shaft into me all the way to the hilt and more I felt my body coalesce on a tide of pleasure the likes of which I had never felt before and that left me screaming against the back of the seat that my face was pressed into.

He was already stretching me so full, only to then constrict tightly around the thickness of his shaft, sent shockwaves throughout me that echoed as loudly as the waves of pleasure that my whole being seemed bathed in.

There came the sure and steady knowledge in the moment that I was going to very much enjoy this man's shaft being placed within me on a regular basis.

My knees collapsed and I slid down flat upon the back of the seat even as he followed along to lay between my legs still fully embedded in me. Conscious thought was beyond me and I groaned as he pulled his shaft out of me.

I felt so empty!

I felt him pulling my shirt up and then it was gone over my head. Feeling groggy with passion and the unevenness of emotion - I wasn't ready for feeling myself rolled to my back and straddled over top of once more.

Opening my eyes, I was in time to see my halter top lifted away and then my eyes flared wide as his mouth formed around my one nipple and suckled hard. Moaning my hands seized his head, but I didn't try to force it away.

I just couldn't imagine the passion that this man had enraptured my body with.

My other nipple fell prey to his lips and moaning I suffered under the torment that he pressed down upon me and then suddenly both my nipples were free to the cool air and his lips were on mine in a kiss that became a possession as his tongue forced my lips apart and plunged into the depths of my mouth to dominantly play with my tongue.

The kiss went on and on and during the length of it, I felt my legs pressed together as he straddled me and then with one hand directing his resurgent shaft I felt him penetrate through my thighs thickly. He didn't enter me, instead he repetitively ground the thick head of his hard shaft into an area just above my opening.

What he was doing felt like heaven and I breathed heavily into his mouth as his manipulation of my intimate anatomy re-awoke my passion to have him inside of me with a vengeance.

Groaning, I felt waves of pleasure suffuse through me again as he continued to rub the head of his shaft against something very sensitive within the reaches of my intimate flesh.

He didn't stop.

He kept surging his hips downward and forcing his shaft through my thighs pressed together by his knees to rub against the same spot again and again and screaming I experienced a second orgasm greater than the first.

Our mouths came free and I sucked in deeply for air as I was in as much need for it as I had been earlier today when I had been held down in the ocean. Mid breath in though his teeth seized ahold of my neck in a sucking clasp, even as his knees split my thighs apart.

My breath left me as my hands clawed into his back as his shaft penetrated all the way back into the core of me on one long wet slide into my tight sheath that made me gasp in both discomfort and the sheer pleasure of having him back within me.

Discomfort was soon gone then, as his shaft repeatedly opened me to his full assault, even as he claimed my hands and pressed them down flat to either side of my head as his lips once more closed over mine stealing away all my air.

There was no stopping my reactions to this man. I clamped down about his shaft again, ever so tightly and with a hard-pressed groan into my mouth, I felt him buck deeper into me and orgasm again.

The passion and feel of him inside of me was so intense that I cried and with a look of franticness he let go of my hands and half rose up off me, but my hands moved down to close over his hips even as I begged, "Don't leave me!"

Relaxing down he buried his face into my neck and exclaimed, "Never!"

We lay there fully connected as our bodies continued to throb in the passion each of us had invoked for each other and I sensed a Divine pairing taking place. My arms came around the plains of Orrin's muscled back and softly I pressed a kiss to his sweaty head still buried against my neck.

For better or worse, he was my man from this day forward and in the moments after all I had just experienced I felt most of my reservations about the divine arrangements by my Creator to be with this man melt away. Truly, he was and could act the beast, but he wasn't all bad and he did care for me.

I continued to hold him to me as completely worn out by my passions and this man's shaft I drifted off to sleep in the midst of a scene of carnage that the world hadn't seen the like of in probably over a thousand years.

CHAPTER THREE

Preparedness

I stood by with an eyebrow firmly raised as I watched Orrin assemble the gear he kept stowed in the back of his Jeep.

Preparedness wasn't the name for it!

This was a man who prepared for the absolute worst.

I had never seen such a complete bug out bag before and if that wasn't enough, he had enough spare items to make virtually an entire second pack of which I would carry.

Very impressed I continued to stand off to the side as Orrin set the extra pack on the ground next to his. He was very quiet this morning, if morning could be what it was called.

The light was dim and yet the evidence of the sun shone through the ash laden clouds overhead dimly in proof of it being morning because of its position in the sky.

Refocusing on Orrin I again wondered at the reason for his quiet reserve. His manner towards me was nothing but respectful though, and so I had little cause to worry.

My face flushed, as the memory of how he had essentially buried his face between my legs this morning and licked me with his tongue, came back in full force of passionate memory.

He glanced at me and noting my blush his brow quirked and he spoke his first words of the day, "Want me to do it again?"

Did I ever, but my response to him was a shy, "No."

He looked away and worked on removing the back floorboard of the Jeep, but in the process of doing so, he said, "I thought you weren't supposed to lie as a Christian."

My face blushed a brighter red, but for a different reason. I didn't give him an answer though and without waiting for one he pulled up the floorboard of the Jeep and I gasped aloud at what was revealed.

"Are you crazy!" I exclaimed, as my eyes took in the arsenal that had been revealed.

"That's what the doctors said." Orrin said nonchalantly and glancing to him I started to disclaim what I'd meant, but holding a hand up, he stated, "I know what you meant."

In the process of doing so he smiled and I was struck by how engaging his smile was.

Feeling a little weak in the knees from the effects of it, I asked, "The doctors said you were crazy?"

"Mentally unstable and prone to uncontrollable bouts of rage is how I believe they put it."

Glancing to me he said seriously, "You were right to fear me."

I shook my head no, and said, "No, I wasn't. I should have prayed sooner is all."

He shook his head and began unloading the stash of weapons. I blinked repeatedly as I saw him connect a string of grenades to his belt.

"Exactly what will they be needed for?" I asked softly.

He glanced at me and then back to his task as he spoke, "Being a civilian and a foreign one at that, I don't expect you to know what even now is occurring. You see I've taken part in disaster training for an event like this and let me tell you the aftermath of an event like this isn't pretty. Those you think should help you will be your executioners in the end."

"What do you mean?"

"You ever hear of FEMA?" He asked and I nodded my head yes.

"Well, there are thousands of FEMA camps in this country. Many are disguised as jails and the irony is that this is exactly what they are. An event like this is something that some very influential people have desperately been waiting for to occur. There are those in this world who feel that there are far too many useless eaters, as they would call them, essentially you and me. A natural event like this gives them the ability to ensure a dramatic drop in population, even as they find popular support to declare martial law and throw the whole book of American freedoms out the door as they sit happily within their underground bunkers swilling down martinis on the rocks while people eat each other on the surface."

The level of bitterness in Orrin's voice was telling and softly I interjected, "You worked for these people?"

"I did. Yes, I played their game for them. To my never-ending shame I confess to being fully complicit with their plans such as they are." He trailed off with before giving me a direct look and stating, "Survivors like you and me without shelter of our own will be rounded up and shipped off to one of those FEMA camps as soon as they catch sight of us. That can never happen. I will put a bullet in your brain before I willingly allow you to enter one of those concentration camps! If for any reason we get separated and authorities of any kind try to coerce you to go with them you resist with everything you've got! They'll tell you that they have food and that you're going to be taken to a safe area, but all that is code for is abuse, starvation, and death, that is, unless you catch the sight of somebody high up and then that would just be never-ending abuse. Do not under any circumstances enter a FEMA camp! The moment you do, you lose all liberties and likely any chance that you had at survival. Do I make myself clear?" He asked firmly and there was no doubting the sincerity of his gaze that demanded an answer from me.

"Understood, Sir. Resist or die trying."

His brow quirked and nodding, he said, "Yes, now take this and keep it with you at all times."

Numbly, I accepted the small 9mm from him along with several clips for it.

"Do you know how to use that?" He asked and surprisingly I did know so I said, "Yes."

"Good. Now I also want you to carry this." He said, leaning what I took to be a shotgun up against my pack.

As for him, he shoved a big looking revolver into his belt and stacked a mean looking semiautomatic rifle up against his pack.

Preparations seemed to be complete and turning to me he crooked a finger and said, "Come here."

Slowly, I did. He swung around me only to clasp his arm about me as his lips whispered into my ear, "Time to be honest, Jolana, and admit you want more. I'd love to strip you down and feast on you again, but we need to be moving. But......"

His hand slipped beneath the loose band of my pants to press heavily against the upper area of the apex of my thighs where I was sensitive the most, only to finish his sentence by saying, "..... there's nothing wrong in making you ache with anticipation to have me again as we walk all day long."

I groaned as the pressure of his finger manipulation of me echoed strongly through the material of my bikini bottom's thin fabric. I was on the verge of something highly pleasurable when he withdrew his hand from stimulating me and groaning, I turned my head to stare at him, but he only smiled as he said, "You've got a long day ahead of you to appreciate everything I'm going to do to you tonight."

He stepped away and I acknowledged to myself that he was indeed a cruel man. I swung on my pack and awkwardly picked up the shotgun and then followed after him as we made our way down off the knoll and into the heart of the destruction wrecked by the tsunami of yesterday.

~~~~~~~
~~~~~~~

Things did not go as planned and the coming night saw us still moving onward. The horror of what we had seen in the course of this day would be forever etched in my memory.

Equally horrible was the reality of Orrin's words coming to full fruition as truth. I had thought he was being a bit too over-the-top in his claims of what authorities would be like to the survivors of such a disaster, but not any longer.

Earlier in the day we had seen another party of survivors and I had been on the verge of asking Orrin if we could team up with them when a helicopter had come up over a rise.

The other party had waved madly at the helicopter and I had been on the verge of doing so as well, when Orrin arrested such a movement by pulling me down to where he had taken shelter behind a trashed car.

The helicopter had circled around to the group and then it had unmercifully opened fire upon them. Gasping, I'd ducked my head against Orrin's chest as the screams of the others had wrung out as they were stalked from above.

Orrin had held me tightly and when the helicopter had gone, he'd patted my back and said, "Time to go, Princess."

It was from that moment onward that I stopped doubting him about anything. The savagery of what life would be like in this fallen world seemed to have doubled in short order.

We saw more survivors as we moved on, but I made no effort to call out to them. Indeed, from my vantage point there would have been no reason to as everyone I saw was scavenging through everything they could find and the setup that Orrin had in readiness would have evoked nothing but covetousness and likely gotten one or both of us murdered.

No, I was very fortunate to be with who I was with. Despite the lack of civil control in the moment I felt safe with him.

In the dark I stumbled wearily and Orrin caught hold of me and stabilized me. "A little farther, Princess. I think I see terrain up ahead that hasn't been touched by the water and indeed I find that encouraging."

Glancing up I peered through the dimness of early morning gloom to see what looked like standing trees up ahead of us, at least I thought I smelled the forest anyway.

Feeling revitalized, by the thought of being surrounded by an unwrecked topography left untarnished by the loss of life and the debris of civilization, I speeded up.

Then at almost the same moment we saw the fires. All along the ridgeline there was the faint glimmer of fires burning into the semi-darkness.

Survivors or governmental authorities?

Did it really matter which?

Orrin stood still and I waited for him to decide the course of action. Turning at last to me he said, somewhat apologetically, "It's going to be light soon. We don't have enough time to slip by whoever they are."

I nodded and he headed off to the side and I followed. He found a sheltered spot where two boxcar trailers had been stacked half on top of the other and unfurling a blanket he unslung his pack and laid down on the blanket.

I did the same and with security I skootched back against his sheltering presence. My eyes closed and it seemed that I was instantly asleep as I felt his one arm come securely around me.

He palmed my one breast in his hand and I smiled wearily as sleep claimed a hold of me. It was a nice feeling to be held by a man.

CHAPTER FOUR

It's a Gift

The sound of loud voices woke me and I sat up startled. There was more sunlight today than there had been yesterday and I looked around in panic as I didn't see Orrin.

My wandering eyes found him toward the one end of the boxcars and my panic instantly stilled. He held one finger up to his lips and I nodded.

Rising up as quietly as I could I walked over to where he stood. Over top of the hood of a tossed car I took in the sight of white trucks and lots of people boarding upon them.

There were men with guns, but for the most part the people seemed happy to go into the trucks. I glanced at Orrin and he whispered, "It's the UN."

I blinked and looked back and my eyes took in the unique characteristic of the blue helmets that some of the soldiers wore. Orrin's conspiracies aside, I had no love for the UN and the sight of them already here on the ground in force only confirmed to me more as to the inconsistencies of what should've been a mass effort to preserve humanity instead of one that seemed bent on the process of extinguishing life rather than saving it.

Glancing to Orrin I took him in fully. This man had kept me from death at least twice now.

He was a good protector and with interest I took in the seriousness of this study of what was going on across the way. He was fulfilling his promise to me in so many ways.

My mind drifted to my promise and then how he'd claimed me and then the following morning of how he had unselfishly showered me with pleasure. Truly, he was a stud and yet he hadn't pressed on me the desire I knew he had for me when we had stopped early this morning.

Instead, he'd held me and let me sleep. Shyly, I regarded him and mulled over the thought of what I wanted to do for him.

Finding the courage to do so was a bit hard to find though.

Sidling up beside him I let my hand close over his groin and squeeze softly. He glanced at me surprised and staring into his eyes deeply, as I rubbed my hand against the expanding flesh beneath his pants, I whispered, "You're a great warrior. Thank you for keeping me safe."

Orrin mumbled out distractedly, "I'm trying, but……."

"No buts. You're doing a great job as my man, honey." I interjected softly.

He swallowed and I watched intensely as vulnerable emotions came to the surface of his eyes and wanting to lock in the changes I saw I whispered, "I couldn't ask for a better man to keep me safe."

"Safe? Who's going to keep you safe from me?" He exclaimed out and smiling I shook my head and said, "I don't need anyone to keep me safe from you, honey."

He seemed to growl deeply and lifting his hand he held it gripped lightly across the front of my throat as he said forcefully, "Do you have any idea how hard I want to take you? I…… I've fought for hours to keep from waking you! I……"

"Go ahead. Take me as hard as you want." I offered challengingly, but he shook his head no savagely and with a soft smile I asked, "Why not?"

"It wouldn't be right. I…… I have no desire to hurt you." He said at the last before looking back off towards the far off slope mostly devoid of people now, even as he let go of my throat.

Smiling, I pressed closer and kissed his neck as I said, "See, I was right. I don't need any other protector other than you."

As I said my words I squeezed my hand as best as I could around the raging shaft that had come to full life behind his pants and with pleasure I saw his eyes close briefly.

Softly then I said, "You know I'm really beginning to suspect that behind your cold hard shell of an exterior that there is a sensitive and loving man buried somewhere in there."

He shook his head negatively and tried his best to ignore me.

Smiling, I undid his belt buckle and as I pulled the zipper of his pants, down I said, "I'm really hungry. Do you mind if I have breakfast?"

His gaze came to me and was one of shock even as I slipped down in front of him to kneel before what I had revealed and stroked to life. I wrapped both my hands around his shaft and felt the thrill of just how big he was.

Glancing up, I said, as I lifted an eyebrow, "You don't mind do you?"

Wiping at his suddenly sweaty brow with a shaking hand, he said, as if to himself, "What did I ever do to deserve this?"

Giving him a serious look I said, "Sometimes Grace is given without measure to those who deserve it least of all."

"Why?" He asked, as I moved my mouth forward toward the beaded drip of moisture that had formed on the head of his shaft.

Glancing up as my lips grazed him I whispered, "Because it's a gift. A gift that is freely given and that can't be earned."

I kept eye contact then with him as my mouth closed fully over the head of his shaft. He shook slightly as my tongue licked the tip of his shaft before then penetrating it slightly.

He groaned and a thrill of pleasure shot through me at the sounding of it. I brought my eyes back to the evidence of his passion for me as I went about discovering the intimacies of a man for the first time.

I let my hands roam and massage upon his thighs all the while keeping my mouth active upon his shaft. Bringing my hands around him I gripped a hold of the cheeks of his bottom and found myself quite enjoying the feel of his muscular bottom that was hard in direct contrast to the soft cheeks of my own bottom.

Touching him and pleasing him had me aching to feel him inside me again, but this moment was about him and I gave unselfishly of myself to further his pleasure in any way that I could.

I felt his balls in the grip of my one hand draw up tighter and with interest I glanced up to view his passion filled face and watch as his mouth fell open even as he filled my mouth with his seed.

I squeezed his balls rhythmically and had the pleasure of feeling him shake as he stood braced with his feet shoulder width apart before me. The taste of him was a bit hard to handle, but it was only right that I should, at least that's how I felt about it.

I swallowed deeply as I did my best to encourage his orgasm to be the best that it could be. His pumping jets of semen spent I let my mouth, pull off of him, only to then lick him clean as I heard his breath puff in and out of him like a blacksmith's bellows.

His beautiful shaft now licked clean I pressed my face forward into the black curly hairs of his groin and breathed in deeply the heavy musky scent of his maleness. I kissed the base of his softening shaft sweetly before popping my head below it to wetly kiss each one of his hairy balls.

That done, I helped pull his pants back up and secure them again.

Glancing up idly I asked, "You don't wear underwear?"

"I like the feel of it without them." He said husky voiced.

My eyebrows quirked at the revealing of that tidbit, but it was him so I accepted it.

Gazing upward, I asked shyly, "Did you like it? I've never made love to a man before."

"Yes!!! I...... why...... why?" He repeated, as he stuttered to frame a question of why I had done what I had.

"Why what?" I asked, turning my head to the side to thoughtfully regard him.

"Why did you make love to me like that?" He breathed out in question.

"Because I wanted to. Why does that shock you? You did it to me."

"I did my best to please you and I loved what I was doing, but what you just did was different. You made me feel special the way you touched me and stuff."

Smiling, I said, as I tilted my head to the other side, "You are special, Orrin. I didn't see that at first, but I do now. Why is it so hard for you to believe that I would do something like what I did?"

"I've never had anyone work to make me feel special like that before."

Smiling tenderly I said, "Well, now you do. Will you please help me up? My knees went to sleep."

He lifted me up and then with sudden passion that was unexpected his hand speared into the hair at the back of my head and held my head steady for his kiss that he pressed upon me with a passion that testified to there being more substance of relationship between us than just the desires of the flesh. My hands rose to frame his face as his kiss stretched on until at long last he broke contact with me.

Something was happening between us and fuzzily I worked on figuring it out.

He let go of me and shakily he wiped at his sweaty brow again before saying, "We should be going."

Feeling bold I piped up with, "But you haven't had your breakfast yet."

He gave me a searing glance before commenting, "Your right I haven't. Come along, honey." He said, as he took my hand and led me back to the blanket that we'd spent the night upon.

The wet ache between my thighs intensified as he pushed me down onto the blanket with a look that said I was about to have a very passionate encounter. A heady thrill shot through me as he kneeled down between my split thighs and began to unclasp my capris.

"Thank you." I whispered.

"My pleasure." He responded back with, and then with an admonishing finger, he said "You're going to need to be quiet though."

"I'll try." I breathed out as my pants and then my bikini bottoms came off.

His arms swept around my bottom and before I knew what to expect he lifted me up to his mouth. My legs naturally curled around the back of his neck even as all my blood rushed to my head as he held me in an inclined downward position.

His mouth descended upon me and it was all I could do not to moan and then as he licked to refrain from screaming.

This was going to be hard!

I heard him chuckle and the feel of the vibrations was just too much and already aroused as I was from pleasuring him I came.

Stuffing my hand against my lips I screamed against it.

Looking down at me he said with a look of wonder, "You are an absolute pleasure!"

With passion lidded eyes, I asked, "Did you enjoy your breakfast?"

"I'm not done yet." He responded back with deeply and I moaned just as deeply as he then proved it to me.

CHAPTER FIVE

Hot Water

It was a relief to move into the cover of untouched vegetation. Already the smells of death and rotting decay were becoming a bit too much to handle.

I'd smelled plenty of dead creatures before, but never like this and what made it all the worse was knowing how many people I was smelling the decomposing remains of. That was especially hard to accept, but inevitable within this new era of chaos.

We walked for hours and skirted away from any sign of human habitation, but soon we would have to cross some congested urban areas. I didn't know what Orrin's plans were but I hoped that they included finding me a new pair of shoes.

The shoes I had were not cut out for this. Indeed, I wasn't sure how cut out for this I was.

The straps of the pack bit hatefully into my shoulders and my back hurt from the weight of the pack, but I didn't complain. Indeed, I felt a bit pathetic as I knew my pack must be half the weight of the one Orrin carried.

That said I couldn't help feeling the way I did.

Tiredly, I switched my grip on the shotgun to my other hand, for the hundredth time.

An electric ripple streaked through the air with a crackle of extreme voltage and I jumped fearfully as the loudest thunderclap I'd ever heard sounded out overhead. More streaks of potent electrical power streaked across the suddenly dark sky overhead.

The force and terrific sound of their booming echoes had me crying out fearfully and trying to cover my ears, but holding the shotgun
made that impossible. My gaze took in Orrin, only to see him scan-
ning about worriedly.

He caught sight of something and then he was seizing my free
hand and yelling, "Come on! We've got to get away from these trees!"

Oh no! I hadn't thought about that.

The reassurance the trees had been for me suddenly vanished as the
reality of being fried to a crisp by being beneath one of them when it
got lit up by a lightning bolt galvanized me into action and gave me
the adrenaline needed to keep up with Orrin as we dashed madly
through the forest.

All of a sudden rain pounded down upon us as if somebody was
pouring buckets of it out from up above.

Instantly soaked I tried my best to keep my footing on the sudden
mush of several inch deep mud that the forest understory soil had become, but it was hard. Orrin more or less was the only thing keeping
me from falling flat on my face.

What he was headed for I could not guess at as I couldn't see anything in the downpour other than his form ahead of me dragging me
onward and the trunks of nearby trees that we were passing by. My
feet touched down on something solid and in the rain pressed darkness
I saw and felt enough to recognize it as a gravel road.

Blearily, I gazed about as the icy chill of the rain began to make its
full impact on me. I saw nothing and then I saw something reflective
looking.

Window glass!

Indeed, it was to this that Orrin drug me onwards to.

The lightning and thunder had never stopped, but had sort of become a background for the rain in a crashing symphony of sound as if
in replication of a World War II tank battle. The battle took new
meaning though, as the ground shook and the sound of wood blowing

apart echoed out behind us in a threatening way of approaching disaster that seemed unstoppable.

Not wanting to, but feeling the need, I glanced back and beheld trees on fire!

How that was possible in this heavy rain, I did not know, but as I looked a bolt of electric blue power streaked down and coalesced a tree into an electric flame the likes of which I'd never seen anywhere before.

Everything in this chaos of a world gone mad had become far more savage than previously before seen.

More and more trees were lit up or blown apart and I turned my head forward and ran with all I had until I was neck and neck with Orrin. The imagery of an alpine like getaway cottage took shape and then the stairs to a second story entrance were before us and we quickly ascended up them.

The place had the appearance of no life to it and I prayed that it was so. The storm was enough to handle right now.

Orrin pushed me beneath an eave of the roof and shivering, I stood there as I thankfully took in the sight of the down strikes of lightning moving off away from us through the forest.

Suddenly I heard glass shatter and clutching my shotgun up to me I held it uncertain as to what to do as my teeth chattered nonstop.

Minutes went by and I was on the verge of going after Orrin when he reappeared uninjured and surprisingly with a smile to say, "No one is here. Come on."

Feeling like my feet were made of lead I did. I stepped through a shattered screen door, mindful of the broken glass on the floor.

The house was dark, but immediately I was struck by the realization that this was a nice place.

Shivering, I stood still upon the hard wood floors feeling slightly at a loss as to what to do as Orrin worked at stretching a canvas tarp out over the door he had broken through.

That done he turned to me and with a curious look he asked, "Why are you just standing there? Get out of those wet clothes, honey."

Coming unglued from my trance I hurriedly took him up on that advice and unslung the hatefully heavy pack from off my shoulders and set my shotgun down to rest against it. Even with fingers fumbling, because of how cold I was, I still managed to get my sodden clothes off in record time.

Orrin had disappeared off to somewhere again. Naked I padded over to lift up a warm fleece blanket from off one end of a couch and with relief I brought it around me, only to then jump with startlemeant as the lights of the house came on.

Staring about the expensive interior of the cottage I searched for a clue as to how electricity had come to life, but found none. I heard a noise and glancing through the balcony railing that showed an overview of the basement level below I saw Orrin reappear from outside through a secondary basement access door.

With a smile he called out, "There's a generator."

I did my best to smile, but my teeth were still chattering.

Orrin bounded up a stairwell and disappeared elsewhere in the house. I gazed longingly towards the comfy looking couch, but I made myself go to an open style kitchen instead.

Opening a cabinet my eyes were blessed with the sight of a fully stocked cabinet full of food.

Closing my eyes, I said out loud, "Thank you God! We so needed this, thank you! I pray for whoever this place belongs to...... I hope they're okay and if not, then I hope and pray that there with You."

My gaze was immediately drawn to a small kitchen table nearby and in particular to the well-worn looking Bible that rested upon it.

I smiled bittersweetly, as I had my answer to the likely outcome of the owners of this getaway in the forest.

As tempting as the food before me was the urge to be dressed warmly was greater. I turned away from the cabinet only to see Orrin standing nearby gazing at me.

He had a thoughtful look on his face and feeling self-conscious I asked, "What?"

"You have a great heart. I mean...... lots of people would thank God for a place out of the rain and for food, but you prayed for the owners of this place. You're different."

I shrugged, feeling a bit embarrassed by the praise I saw in his eyes and said, "I'm just who God made me to be."

"No. You've made choices. Good choices."

That was true to some extent, but not knowing how to respond I didn't say anything.

Crooking his finger, he said with a sudden grin, "Come this way, Baby Girl."

He disappeared and I followed along finding myself increasingly enamored by this softer side of the man I had thought of as only being cruel natured and hard of heart.

Following along, I soon heard the sound of water apart from that which was sheeting off the eaves of the house.

With delight, I followed Orrin into a resplendent master bathroom that had a shower that looked like it belonged in a spa resort. Steam rose from off the water falling from multiple jets and with a squeal of delight, I dropped the fleece blanket and jumped into the streams of hot pulsating water.

The water was quite hot, but I didn't mind, in fact I craved its heat. Gazing up into the flow of it with my eyes closed I soaked in the feel of it cascading down over me with forceful warmth.

The feeling of being made clean again when the world outside seemed nothing else but dirty and torn apart seemed in a way to rejuvenate my soul.

My skin prickled with surprise and desire as the feel of a fully aroused man of hard-core conditioning stepped up to press against me from behind.

Turning my back to the flow of water I shyly pressed my face into his curly chest hairs as the sensation of being with a man in the intimacy of an act such as showering together caused tingles to sweep up and down my spine.

He pulled on my hair and letting my head fall back, I accepted his kiss as the warmth of the shower warmed me up on the outside, even as the reaction to his kiss did the same to me from within.

I moaned regretfully as he pulled his lips away from mine. Opening my eyes, I took in the sight of him picking up a soap bar and then to my delight he began to wash me with it.

I stood, as if transfixed, as his sudsy hands moved over and under my breasts caressingly and then to my sides and stomach. Turning me he washed my back and I moaned as the feeling of him doing that seemed to make a dream come true within my heart.

I blushed against the heat of the water as I heard him kneel down in the shower, only to then feel his lips kiss one of the cheeks of my bottom. My face got redder still at the feel of the soapy bar moving upon my bottom and then up and down through the cleft of my cheeks.

The intimacy of his touch was breathtaking and I pressed my hands against the shower's wall for support as he continued to wash me by gliding his soapy hands down the backs of my thighs and around to the front of them.

Languidly I stood still as the heady desire for this man threatened to consume me with the urge I had to feel him pulsating within me.

Finishing my feet he rose up to press against me commandingly from behind. I thought he was going to take me and I was only too willing to bend over for him to do so, only he surprised me again by spearing his hands full of a rich smelling shampoo into my hair.

I moaned at the feel of his fingers massaging along my scalp and gliding through my hair. The feeling was indescribable and I felt like my voice was one long drawn-out moan of delight.

He chuckled near my ear and said, "You really like this."

He had no idea what he was doing to me!

In this moment I was putty for whatever he could possibly wish to do to me.

I'd never felt so cherished or loved before and I ached to be able to return the appreciation I felt from him for me in some way. He washed my hair clean of the shampoo and feeling as if I had a chance to return the favor I grabbed a hold of the soap bar and muscled him as best as I could into the direct flow of water.

Gazing at him with all the love I was coming to feel for this hidden gem of a man I said playfully lifting the soap bar, "My turn."

He smiled and with pleasure I began to soap up the muscled plains of his chest and shoulders. I scrubbed beneath his arms and then with delight at the anticipation I saw upon his face I rubbed the soap bar into his curly pubic hairs even as my sudsy hand washed up and down his shaft that had stayed in full vigor of erectness with its desire to plunder my body.

The time for that was coming, but I wanted to finish washing him first. Kneeling down before him I leaned forward and placed a kiss on the head of his shaft.

Glancing up, then I said, "Turn around big boy."

He did so reluctantly.

I was faced with his rear and far from being repulsed by it; I was both intrigued and turned on by the tight strength of it as I washed him as thoroughly and as intimately as he had me.

Leaning forward I pressed a kiss to each of his tight cheeks before moving on to wash his legs one by one. Standing up I washed his back and felt turned on all over again by the feel of just how strong he was.

Getting the shampoo I doused his head with it and then with relish, because some deep buried feminine part of me knew how much I was tormenting him I pressed into him from behind, as I stood up on tip-toe, to run my hands through his thick oily hair.

As I massaged his scalp in a rhythmic motion the full essence of my breasts brushed and repeatedly ground against the tensed muscles of his back. I brought his head under the water and washed it clean and then I let go of the beast as with delighted anticipation I waited for him to seize a hold of me and make me his.

Turning and sending water everywhere his large hands gripped a hold of me and brought me near for his kiss that was truly savage. I knew that I'd aroused something to a fever pitch within him and I didn't object at all to the roughness of his touch as I knew he needed release.

His lips left mine and his hands spun me around in the shower.

Bravely I brought my hands to rest against the shower wall as I bent forward for him, but he pressed on my shoulders demandingly and I realized that he wanted me to move more.

Willingly I bent over at the direction of his hands, until I had nothing to grasp hold of but my own ankles. I did so and closed my eyes as his thick shaft pressed into my wetness in a commanding way that screamed of his sharp need for a release.

Submissively I did my best to be that open vessel in order to fulfill his every want. I gasped, but held onto my ankles as his shaft gored all the way into me thickly and with his hands firmly gripped about my waist he let me have it.

There was no thought of my pleasure in this moment and that was fine. I closed my eyes against the discomfort and did my best to keep my balance on my feet as he rammed his shaft fully and deeply into me each time in a way that stated I was his and indeed I was.

He shoved deeply into me and hearing him cry out with real pleasure I felt his shaft pulse within me with the power of his orgasm and outpouring of seed.

His orgasm was a long one, but almost instantly upon its conclusion he was pulling on my hair to bring me upright.

Blood rushing out of my head, I did come upright enough to rest my hands against the wall again, as he continued to pulse passionately within me with an erection that wouldn't go away even after it had achieved its completion. He was such a stud!

I relished the feel of him, resting against my back and feet apart, I partially supported him in the shower through the weakness caused by his sharp release of passion into me.

Breathing heavy against my neck, he mumbled out as warm water continued to rain down over both of us, "Sorry. Selfish. I......"

In an action meant to interrupt him I bucked my bottom into his groin and his still partly seated shaft moved within me and with a groan his hands formed over my hips.

Glancing over my shoulder I said with earnestness, "I'm not complaining. I'm here. I'm yours. Have your way with me however you like, honey. I trust you and I know you have my best interests at heart."

"You do?"

"I do!" I affirmed before erotically shifting my rear into him in a playful manner.

He groaned, and shaking his head, he exclaimed, "I wish there were more people like you!"

Smiling, I said, "Well, you can choose to be someone like me, anytime that you wish to."

With seriousness he said, "I might just do that."

Turning my head forward I earnestly prayed on the spot that he would indeed do that. He withdrew his shaft and straightening up I pressed back against him and relished the feel of his arms come around me from behind to hug me tightly.

He pressed his face against my hair and it took me a moment to realize that he was crying.

My heart felt overwhelmed as I heard the sounds of repressed emotion finally coming up to the surface of this toughest of the tough.

Coasting my hand soothingly over his arms gripped tightly about me, I did the one thing I could think to do at the moment, I sang.

Feeling a give in the tension of his arms I made to turn around and he let me, but as I did so he collapsed to his knees and not wanting to show his tears he ducked his face in against my belly as his arms hugged around the back of my thighs.

Gently, but firmly I pulled his head back until I could gaze into his crying eyes.

With passion I said, "I'm here for you. I'm not going anywhere. You cry all you want. If you want to talk, we'll talk. You can tell me anything, anything at all and I won't think the less of you. I'm yours, Orrin. If you want to bend me over again and take me hard then let's do it or if you want me to make sweet love to you then I will. You say it and we'll do it, honey. Okay?"

He nodded and then pressing his face back against the softness of my belly. I heard him mumble out, as his grip around me grew tighter again, "I want you to hold me."

My hands swept around the back of his head and I pressed him more fully to me. He turned his head to the side and with one hand holding his head to me and the other massaging upon his forehead and face I began to sing again.

I sang love songs, Christian praise songs, my favorite songs and I did so until the water began to get cold.

I turned it off and then I coaxed him up to his feet and dried him off, as well as myself, and then led him into the bedroom that matched the bathroom for opulence.

Pulling the covers of the plush looking bed back, I pressed him down to sit upon it and then with a loving smile I kneeled down before him and pressing his thighs apart.

I made love to his resurgent member with my mouth and hands until he came hard with an explosive release of his seed into my mouth. Swallowing his essence I rose up and kissed him full on the lips in a way that gave him a taste of his own seed that I hadn't licked away completely yet from off my lips.

I wanted him to know that I accepted him as he was and that my heart was such as to please him, only him.

Pulling back from the kiss I pressed him down and crawling in beside him I pulled at him until he rolled onto his side and rested his head on my chest that made a soft cushion for him.

Pulling the covers up I folded my arms around him and held him tightly as he started to cry again and when that was done he began to talk and I listened. I listened for hours and never once did I let go of him or pass a judgmental word down upon him for any of the secret things he told me about.

In short, I loved him unconditionally and he sensed it and with his consciousness bared to the full he fell asleep against me.

Still holding him, I stared up at the dark ceiling as the rain continued to pound outside.

This man had done much that was awful and yet his heart was burdened by those things and not accepting of what he had done. He was a man I sensed who was willing to change.

He was a man worth fighting for.

Feeling tears come to my own eyes, I whispered into the darkness, "Thank you God for helping me take this option. I can't be everything for him, but what I can be of help in please help me to be so, while at the same time I pray that Your, Holy Spirit wouldn't give up on him, but instead I pray that You will press upon him to make the changes and commitments that he needs to. Help me be whatever part of that process that I can be and thank you again for a man who loves me, even though he hasn't said as much, I still know that he does, but truly it's Your love that he sees because I at first hated him, only to now see what You saw all along. Thank you for never giving up on us lost souls. To You be all the glory and honor for what I know You are going to do in this man's life and in mine."

My prayers and praises said I fell into a contented slumber as my mates head lay one day where our baby's head would one day lay. I was sure about very little in this upturned world on fire, but one thing I knew that would occur would be that there would be children.

Not just one either. How many I didn't know, but they would all be with this man, who at first had terrorized me, but now held me in his sleep as if I was the most precious thing in the world.

CHAPTER SIX

Caution Taken

The smell of food awoke me and with my stomach crying out for it, I sat up in the bed. The bed was empty and yet the smell of food gave proof positive to the testament of where my lover was.

Getting up I searched the room's closet and with delight, I spied a long-sleeved man's plaid shirt. I slipped it on and the tales of it came down to mid thigh in their coverage of me.

Grinning, I glanced away from the mirror as I finished buttoning the loose fitting shirt up. Orrin wouldn't be able to resist me and for me that was quite all right.

I stepped free of the bedroom with a smile of anticipation, but abruptly froze at the sight of a large German Shepherd with teeth bared facing down Orrin, who held a chair at the ready to brain the dog if need be. The dog's deep-seated growl was ugly to hear as was its aggressiveness to us.

The dog looked well fed, but on what was the question. We were but days from a disaster of the former civilized order and yet this dog acted like it had been born wild.

Actually, it seemed worse as I think a wolf would've had the good sense to leave and look for easier food elsewhere.

Then to make matters worse a second dog slipped in past the canvas covering the doorway soon to be followed by another and another.

All four were well fed looking and yet their demeanor towards Orrin was one of intenseness that said they wished to kill just for the sake of killing. They all exhibited a clear bloodlust in their actions as they all closed in on Orrin, who now gave ground until his back was pressed up to the railing of the balcony.

My man was in danger and quite without hesitation despite the threat I tiptoed forward and reached down for the shotgun that I'd left in the middle of the floor leaning up against my pack. I'd been a girl of fifteen the last time I'd shot clay pigeons with my brothers, but the mechanics of the shotgun were still clear to me.

I shucked a shell forward even as my thumb pushed the safety off. All four slobbering jawed gazes of the assorted dog breeds gathered within our haven switched to me and I pulled the trigger.

One dog went flying and the other three attacked when they should've all gone for cover. Something was clearly not right with these formerly domesticated animals.

Shucking the spent shell free I blasted away again as I depressed the aim of the shotgun downward at the fast approaching dogs. Two went sprawling about on the floor, but the fourth had launched for me with teeth bared.

I fell to the floor and as I hit the ground on my side, I shucked the shotgun again and as the dog landed down beyond me, I let him have it and with a squeal he plopped over dead on the floor as blood sprayed up against the wall beyond him. Quickly rising up I turned and sent a shell into each of the two dogs whining and growling upon the floor in their incapacity to attack me instead of their one thought being of escape as it should have been.

At the firing of the last shell the house fell eerily silent and breathing heavy I looked for Orrin. He was coming closer to me skirting around the dogs on the floor as he did so.

Taking the shotgun from me he laid it on the kitchen countertop and I willingly stepped into his arms and for the first time I felt how bad I was shaking as his arms closed about me tightly.

Against my hair I heard him say, as his hands reached down and dipped beneath the hem of the shirt to grip the cheeks of my bottom, "You're quite the girl, Jolana."

Pulling back enough to gaze up at him, as his fingers squeezed intimately with their hold upon me, I said preemptively, before the passion to have me came to full life in his eyes, "I'm hungry."

Laughing he let go of my bottom and said, "Yes, ma'am. I'd better see that my little, Annie Oakley doesn't get too hungry or you might air my hide out with some pellets."

"Who is Annie Oakley?"

"Old American history. Here, how about you go back to the bedroom and I'll bring your food to you so we don't have to be around these dead mutts while we eat."

I nodded and let go of him. He stepped away, but stopped as I said, "The dogs……. I think they've turned. I mean………" I left the rest of my thought unsaid, as I really didn't want to commit to the idea of what might be going on.

With seriousness he said, "Say what you're thinking."

Haltingly then I said, "In the Bible it says that in the last days that the beasts of the field will turn on mankind. These dogs weren't hungry and they've only been without human interaction for a few days. Look they all have tags and collars. Even the severe trauma of these past few days hasn't been enough to turn them into the killers that these dogs were. I…… I'm just saying maybe that's why these dogs were like this and if that's the case, then how much else out there in the forest is going to come hunting after us? How will we ever survive if all animal life has suddenly gone mad with the desire to kill us?" I stated at the last with real fear as the enormity of all that could mean came to full life within my mind as an unfolding horror.

Orrin shrugged, "I'm not concerned by that if that is the case."

"Why not?" I exclaimed.

"As long as I keep your shotgun full of shells I know that I'll be safe." He said with dry humor.

I rolled my eyes dramatically and to the tune of Orrin's grin I headed back to the bedroom.

~~~~~~~~

Orrin

Orrin watched her go and kept his grin in place until she was gone from view. The grin slid from off his face entirely, then and with seriousness and a sense of despair, he turned his gaze to the four bloody dogs lying upon the floor.

She was right. Something very odd was up with the animals, at least as evidenced by these dogs.

The imagery of cougars and grizzly bears all the way down to the smallest mutant Chihuahua coming out at them with the same bloodlust that these dogs had exhibited sent a shiver of apprehension down his spine.

Wiping his hand across his brow at the sudden cold sweat, he felt there he then looked about before gazing upward and stating, "How am I going to keep her safe? She believes in You and she's like perfect and yet what right is there in her getting chewed up? I'm only one man! I........ I need help. I don't want her hurt! Please. Please help me keep her safe! I would be very grateful and...... well, I would be very grateful."

Orrin turned awkwardly away from his first conversation with God, since he had been a boy of eleven years of age. That former time had been marked by one of angry outrage, as he had screamed, at the God in heaven who had allowed his mother, who had believed in Jesus, to die.

Orrin had never pursued another moment with the God, whom his mother had placed her faith in, until today, because in so many ways, if not far more ways, Jolana meant more to him than even his mother had to him as a boy.

Turning away and trying not to dwell on how helpless he felt at keeping the woman he had come to love safe he fetched her plate of food and a cup of juice and headed for the bedroom.
~~~~~~~~

One thing was certain. They could not stay here.

Very clearly he felt the urge of something telling him to keep moving on into the interior and leave this house of comforts and abundant food behind.

Was the urging within his spirit caused by God trying to tell him something?

Why would God help him of all people when it came to that?

He wasn't sure, but he wished he knew just the same. Nevertheless the urge was such that before the day advanced much further he intended to be on the move.

Jolana would not be happy, but he had to do what was right and denying this instinctual urge to move on in the name of staying in a place of comfort was simply not the right thing to do.

CHAPTER SEVEN

"It shows."

The last pack of food made I slung the satchel over my shoulder and made my way downstairs and through the basement door to where Orrin was packing away the supplies onto the four-wheel-drive gator that he'd discovered in a shed near the house.

I gazed a bit mutinously at him, as I watched him stow away the supplies and tools that we had scavenged from the house and its surroundings in the last two hours.

We hadn't even made love this morning and within a few more minutes of time we would be leaving this cozy spot that had given us refuge from the storm. Feeling convicted, though for my errant thoughts because of the angst I felt for the open forest and what terrors it might hold, I focused on putting my trust in Orrin in that he was doing the right thing.

He took the pack of food from me and began securing it down.

Not looking up, he said, "I'm sorry we have to leave, but I feel it's for the best. Something isn't right and I feel like we need to get inland farther."

He glanced up at me and I dutifully nodded my assent to his plan.

He glanced down and then said, "Something else. Have you noticed how much colder it is today?"

I had noticed that, but I really hadn't given it a lot of thought other than to dress myself warmly. I started to ponder on the unseasonal occurrence of the coldness now though.

Speaking my thoughts I asked, "Do you think with all this ash and other factors that an end to summer and the beginning of an early on-set of winter has begun?"

"The idea has crossed my mind. Not only that, but I know to some degree that an event of something like a mini Ice Age has been ex-pected for a long time and has been extensively planned for by the elite. We've just recently within the past two years entered a solar minimum where the sun will put out less heat than typical for about the next 15 or 30 years. The global elite I used to work for knew about it and to some degree have viewed it as a global reset button by which to help thin the masses so to speak. I never gave it much thought as I really didn't care about living or dying, but now it's different. There's you. You and your belief in God make everything different!" He said with emphasis, as he finished tying off the canvas he had stretched over the mountain of supplies and tools that we had confiscated from the premises and packed onto the bed of the four-wheel-drive gator.

I smiled at him warmly and when he glanced over at me again, I asked, "So we head south for warmer country?"

Surprisingly, he shook his head no before saying, "You don't want any part of what is going to happen in the warmer regions with every-body fighting over limited resources and trampling over each other for continued breath. It will be a madhouse of humanity falling apart at the seams. No, we head inland and look for higher ground."

"You want to go higher in elevation? Won't that be colder still?"

"Yes and no. Yes, it will be cold, but there should be more sunlight and so at times it will be warmer than in the shaded valley bottoms below and if you're right about the animals then it will be to our bene-fit to be somewhere inhospitable and less likely for them to stick around in."

It made sense in a way I guess, but still I didn't like the idea of be-ing cold. Still, as an option, it was better than being either eaten by former pets or extinguished by one of my own kind.

"With proper rationing I think we've got nine months to a year's worth of food here and if we can find more along the way all the better."

"Do you have a destination in mind?"

"I'm not sure how far off we are or exactly where we are when it comes to that, but in that general direction I know there is a ski resort." He said, pointing off towards the northwest before continuing with, "I've stayed at a mountain cottage there before and I know there's a good supply of firewood and when I was there a couple years back they were well stocked with food."

Just then there was the sound of a dog barking in the distance followed by another and another farther off still from the sound of the first one. Orrin and I shared a glance and without a word I slipped around to the passenger seat and hopped in and buckled up.

Leaning forward I picked up the shotgun resting against the dash and laid it across my lap, which was a comfort to me all of its own.

I sensed Orrin looking at me and glancing his way I saw him bemusedly glancing from me to the shotgun and back again.

"What?" I asked defensively, but he said nothing as he shook his head and eased into the driver's seat of the 4 x 4. He eased it forward onto the trail that led further into the forest and away from our haven.

His hand came over and patted my knee and speaking loudly I heard him say, "I feel safer having you along."

I thought he was joking at first, but his face was serious, as he chartered a way forward as fast as the rough terrain would allow. I glanced back and in the distance I saw fast moving dots of four-legged color scrambling up the stairs of the house.

Were the creatures being affected with madness, specifically being ordered by some entity to seek out human habitation and destroy its occupants?

Who knew, it was hard to say, but I found myself suddenly very grateful to be on the move instead of back at the house fending off hordes of former pets gone bad.

I glanced over at Orrin lovingly and let my hand settle over the top of his thigh and squeezed warmly. He glanced my way and I gave him a smile that promised more, which was a mistake as we almost ran headlong into a tree.

Recovering at the last moment Orrin swerved around the tree, but then gruffly said, "Don't distract me like that!"

"I didn't say a thing." I admonished back at him.

With a sigh, he said, "You don't have to. The act of you simply breathing is a distraction."

"You want me to stop?" I asked playfully, but there was no playfulness in the serious tone of his response of, "No!"

~~~~~~~

It was cold! There was little left to doubt that the weather was indeed radically changing by the hour.

How many miles we had come I did not know, but the ski slopes in question now lay visible in the far-off distance. We would not reach them today though.

At various times we had come across bands of people, but we had managed to avoid detection so far from them. Universally, all the people were fleeing from the higher ground that we were heading for.

Their actions seemed like a good idea, but more and more I was coming to trust the instincts of my man rather than that of a popular group consensus. God had given me a good caretaker for sure.

Just then a snowflake fell down before my eyes. Snow in July!

Glancing over at Orrin I asked with a shiver as more and more's snowflakes began to fall, "When are you going to stop for the night?"

Orrin shook his head negatively and said, "I'm not. This snow, I have a feeling it's not going to stop anytime soon and this thing isn't cut out for deep snow."
~~~~~~~

Glancing over at me he took in my blue lips and reaching his arm out to lay across my shoulders, he pulled me closer and said, "I'm sorry."

I wasn't sorry though. I had a man who cared enough for me to sacrifice of himself and push himself to the edge to better our chances of survival. What more could a girl ask for than that?

"When do you think we'll get there?"

"Sometime in the early morning I think. I hope anyway. Try to get some sleep."

I glanced down at the dusting of snow already accumulated across the hood of the 4 x 4. Would we get there in time or would we get hung up in the snow?

I didn't want to think about that. Pressing my face into his shoulder I huddled under the blankets more and closed my eyes to the grimness of what our continued struggle for life would be like.

I let Orrin face the future alone as I closed my eyes and gave in to the desire for sleep and escape from the reality of the moment.

~~~~~~~~

The screeching whine of our tires and the back and forward jerks of the vehicle had me coming awake startled. It was very dark and even colder than before.

It was very cold!

I couldn't feel my feet at all, but my face was halfway warm from where I had been nestled up against Orrin's side. I glanced to Orrin and gasped as I took in the ice frozen to his beard stubble.

Glancing away from him I took in the reality of our situation. The snow was now deep and he was having to literally back up the 4 x 4 and then ram it forward in order to make any headway at all through it.
~~~~~~~~

How he could see anything at all in the dark and through the falling snow was beyond me as the headlights of the vehicle were uselessly covered over with snow.

What time it was I did not know, but it was late.

I clutched onto the handrail as he surged forward again with all tires spinning as the 4 x 4 pushed up a snow drift ahead of us. Glancing down I saw that we were almost out of fuel.

I glanced back only to see that the extra fuel jugs were jiggling about softly in evidence of how empty they were.

When had he stopped to fuel up?

How had I slept through so much?

Feeling guilty I looked about for what I could do, but found nothing to do at the moment, but pray and pray I did. It seemed that we were on a narrow road and managing to crest over a ridge Orrin plunged down over it recklessly as he used the downward momentum of the 4 x 4 to plow through the snow.

He'd driven all night through this!

Unbelievably, I saw a structure take shape in the gloom of what I realized were the first moments just before sunrise.

He plowed the 4 x 4 through the heavy snow until literally it was hung up on the snow with all four tires spinning.

It didn't matter though, because we had reached our objective.

With a groan of effort Orrin stiffly came unglued from his place behind the wheel and stepped out into the deep pressed whiteness still falling heavily from the sky. He stumbled and fell down in it, but feeling revived I hopped out after him and exerting everything I had in me I tugged him back up and together we struggled our way through the snow to the solid wooden door of a snug looking log cabin.

The door was of course locked, but pulling out a knife Orrin jammed it between the door lintel and the door's lock and the door popped open. We fell inside into the dark, gloomy interior of the cabin sending snow everywhere.

Finding a flashlight in my pocket that I'd taken from the house I switched it on and quickly made out the structure of a fireplace.

I left Orrin on the floor and going to the fireplace I went about making a fire of the readily available kindling stacked up nearby.

It took a little bit for the fire to draft, but it caught on steadily and shivering so hard that I was half afraid my teeth would crack I added more wood steadily to it.

A real blaze fired up and I laid the dry wood to it until the fireplace was full.

The heat being let off by the blaze was indescribable, but I tore myself away from the warming pleasure of it and went to Orrin.

Grabbing his hands, I tugged him across the floor, until he lay in front of the fire.

He was passed out, but breathing. Wiping at the sweat on my brow caused by the exertion of moving him I faced the situation of discerning what he would do if he could.

Steeling myself to the cold I headed back outside and floundered through the snow drifts to get back to the 4 x 4 and then I began to unpack it of all of its contents.

Perhaps what I was doing was unnecessary, as the 4 x 4 wasn't going anywhere, but it's what I knew Orrin would do if he was able to.

I made trip after trip back into the house, only taking the time to add wood to the fire and check on Orrin. The cabin was getting quite warm now.

I made my last trip out and grabbed up, among other things my shotgun. I made my way back through the channel I had made through the snow feeling proud of what I had achieved.

Gaining my way to the door of the cabin I stopped to face the brightening sky of the morning sunrise. Still it continued to snow on.

Our tracks to this haven on the upper slope of a ski resort were completely obscured by freshly fallen snow and I had a deep sense of awareness that we were the only two people anywhere in the nearby vicinity, which included the ski resort and many other cabins just like our own.

A sense of peace and of being divinely watched over by an all-powerful Creator filled me with joy and smiling I said, "Thank you, Father!"

Still smiling I entered the cabin that was now fairly roasting and shut the door. I shut the dead bolt closed even as the snow outside provided its own form of security in keeping us safe from humanity trying to save itself from the elements as well as its own kind.

There was no struggle for life here though. In this little cabin and indeed in all the other cabins and the ski resort itself we would no doubt find everything we needed in order to survive.

My man had been very wise to come here.

Going to Orrin I saw that he was awake.

He was staring at the flames of the fire and his eyes were full of tears, but as I came near the look he gave me was one full of joy. I knelt down beside him and raising his hand up he caressed his fingers down my jaw as he said, "Thank you for helping me find the way home. I promised God that if He would get me through to a place where you would be safe that I would give my life to Him and ask for His forgiveness for everything that I've done wrong. I've done that and it's largely because of your witness to me that has helped bring me through the darkest tunnel of my life and back into the light I knew as a child, when my mother taught me of God and of the redeeming grace to be found in His Son, Jesus. Thank you for being who you are, Jolana! You're quite a girl."

Crying openly with hard-pressed joy I seized his hand and kissed the palm of it before saying, "I'm your girl! I'll always be your girl!"

Looking overcome he whispered, "I know. Truly, God is good."

"Yes, He is!" I affirmed, as I kneeled down over him to kiss him with all the passion and love I had for him.

It wasn't enough, though!

I wanted him inside me. I wanted to mark this day, this moment of joy, by being as close to him as I possibly could be and to that end, I broke our kiss off and tore at his clothing that had just begun to thaw out.

By the heated blaze of the fire I uncovered him, until in its heated glow he lay bare. I tore at my own clothes and he helped me and then rising up over him I welcomed his shaft all the way into the special haven that had been created just for him within my body.

Breathing heavy I leaned forward onto my elbows so that our hearts touched each other and I kissed him all over again as his hands stroked over the curves and hollows of my body meant for only him to take pleasure in.

I couldn't bring myself to move upon his shaft buried deeply within my core, as I didn't want to part myself from his indwelling presence within me for even the slightest of moments and yet I ached for his possession of me.

Seeming to sense my dilemma Orrin's hands came to my hips and he held me tight to him as he proceeded to shift his hips up and down and slam his shaft deeply within me.

My body rose and fell to the tune of his thrusts up into me in a clear testament to the strength of my man. Breaking our kiss I let my face fall against his neck as my body went over the edge of the orgasm that he had stroked to life within my inner being.

Crying out I bit into his shoulder as the passion he gave me only intensified with each stroke of his shaft up into me. Truly, I could ask for no more in life than what I had been gifted with in the form of this man, of which I was glad to live out the rest of my days with in the blissful harmony of being his.

I came again and so did he and with relish I felt the insides of my sheath massage and constrict lovingly around his shaft as he took the hard-won pleasure that he deserved from bringing my own body to the heights of passion and beyond.

Exhausted, but with my heart pounding, I lay still upon the body of my mate as his hands lovingly flexed around the shapes and contours of my body in direct contact with his.

I don't know how much time had passed by when I heard him whisper, "Jolana?"

Bringing my head up I met his gaze, only to read the full sincerity of it, as he said, "I love you."

Suddenly crying, I blubbered out past my emotions spilling out all over his chest and said, "I love you, too!"

Softly smiling, he said, "It shows."

His hand stroked across my cheek and adoringly I pressed my face into it. I gazed into his eyes for several long moments before I looked around and then gazed into the fire as a deep-seated happiness invaded every last part of me.

"What are you thinking?" He asked smiling.

Turning my gaze to him I playfully said, "Oh, I was just imagining all the ways that I could think of to experience pleasure with you."

"Oh really? Tell me what comes to mind?" He said playing along with an easy joy that bespoke of the fact that he felt as free as I did in this moment just be ourselves with each other, with nothing held back.

Leaning forward I whispered into his ear and then drawing back, I laughed at the look of playful shock upon his face.

Instantly I felt his shaft come alive against the flesh of my inner thigh.

Pushing up I winked down at him before saying, "But first you have to catch me."

I started to move away quickly, but before I knew it, I found myself grasped ahold of and deposited firmly upon the floor where he had just been as he even now leaned down over me aggressively.

Sighing playfully I breathed out, "Oops. Yuh, got me!"

Shaking his head while softly laughing, he said, "You're too much. I seriously don't deserve you. That said; however, I'm never going to let you go!"

Smiling with all the joy I felt I willingly allowed myself to become his prisoner of delight. As he stretched my legs upward toward my head, I grasped my own ankles and pulled them the rest of the way.

I wanted him in this way, because the more I experienced of him, the more I realized that I had been created to take him deep.

His hands covered over mine and with my feet pressed to the bed to either side of my head, his shaft stroked home within me and I cried out with an abandoned joy at the feel of my man as deep as he could literally go inside of me.

Truly the world outside had gone to hell, but right here - right now - nothing had ever felt so right as he did buried within me.

I breathed out, "I love you!" Over and over again, as he slid into me over and over again, until we were both lost in the passion that we had for each other, and there was nothing left to do but feed the fire and stay warm within each other's arms.

Orrin and I were a pair and with God's help we would both survive and flourish in the new harsh reality that the world had taken on outside. I felt sure of it even as my faith in God testified of it and now I wasn't alone in my faith, but together we were two equal halves of a whole.

We were now of one flesh and with God's help we were capable of meeting any challenge in life that was thrown against us.

THE END

Dear Reader,

I hope you enjoyed Jolana's story Sometimes we really do need to take our hands off the steering wheel and trust what God has for our lives over what we may already have planned. There's no guarantee that things will work out in a way that we want them to, but God's way is always the best way – always! This series features books that are standalone reads. There simply stories of couples placed in extreme circumstances. The First Chapter Excerpt for *Peril without Mercy*, Book 2 of Apocalypto, starts on the next page. I hope you enjoy!

Author's Corner

It would seem that the genre of Erotic Christian Fiction, which I have coined in terms of labeling what I have written, appears to be an entirely new avenue within the Fiction market. Many, who call themselves 'Christian' will not understand what I have taken upon myself to do and in general I expect reactions to what I've written to be hostile and that's okay. Why is that okay? The reason it is okay is because it is better to do what God says then stay hidden safely away within the mass of a group and only do what is perceived amongst the group as 'okay'. Truly the path to hell is paved with both the 'doctrines of man' and 'group think'. I write what I do, because I follow the leading of the Holy Spirit of God and nothing else. This avenue of Christian Erotic themed fiction is something He laid upon my heart to do and I chose to obey the calling and go wherever He wanted it to go. It is within my heart to be obedient to God always and to that end I have gone farther than I ever expected to be asked of me by my God in terms of witnessing to a lost and dying world, but even so, His will be done. If you have questions or comments, please feel free to direct them to me at the following email address: I don't always have answers, but I can pray for you and whatever I can't do – God can.

author-aedan-sayla@proton.me

Thanks for reading and please do leave a review!

Peril without Mercy – Book 2 of Apocalypto

Chapter One

Would nothing ever be the same again?

The answer was - No!

Grimly, I glanced away from the mile-long line of people waiting for a handout of food from the FEMA wagons.

Once again I made myself the promise that I would not be one of those people.

I hurried on, but as usual, my appearance in town attracted notice, because I always brought food with me. Fresh food and not the pre-packaged salt bricks that FEMA passed out.

What the long-term effects of consuming such prepackaged food would be I did not want to speculate as to.

The desire for something better than it already had people clamoring about me offering anything and everything by means of payment for what I carried in the sack on my back, but shouldering past them, I stepped up the stairs of the town's surviving church that had been turned into an orphanage and made my way inside leaving them behind.

Once again, I was surrounded by a clamoring mob, but this time I didn't mind.

Pastor Joseph Orndorff glanced up from where he sat at a desk and gave me a broad smile and said by way of greeting, "Bless you, Adam! This is your second trip to town this week! Things going better with the plantings than you anticipated?"

"They are believe it or not. Must be your prayers doing it though." I responded back with as I passed off the heavy sack of food to him.

He took it and with his other hand, he squeezed my arm as saying in a softer tone of voice not meant for the kids to hear, "Thank you, Adam. You know how I hate to feed them that garbage from the wagons."

I ducked my head down and shrugged as I turned to view the room full of excited kids of varying ages ranging from toddler to preteen now filled with joy at the prospect of eating something good for dinner.

"Don't mention it." I said softly.

Pastor Joseph patted my back hard, "I will most definitely mention it before God tonight! You're a living angel, Adam!" He said, before moving off with the bag into the inner reaches of the church that nobody for the most part wished to attend anymore.

To a large degree within the minds of the community God had failed them and so they had moved on to make the best of what was the toughest of situations.

A poor choice in my opinion, as life without God, in my opinion really wasn't worth the living.

A few others felt that way, but that was it, just a few. The rest of the town of Transum, Oklahoma were out to survive the apocalypse of our time by any means at their disposal.

The fireballs that had destroyed life as we knew it had come just two years ago. The countryside had been decimated, with the cities a sheer disaster of unimaginable horror the likes of which kept one up at night and spurred the need to carry a gun. That is if guns were allowed.

Any gun seen was confiscated on the spot and its owner denied food rations for two weeks.

Needless to say every gun within the county had disappeared a long time ago into one of the white vans that made continuing circuits about the land doling out there prepackaged food meant to survive a millennia if need be.

No, life would never be the same. All there was to do now was to make the best of it and seeing that these children had something good to eat for the moment was my best attempt at doing so.

I cared far less for the adults, who roamed the town, as they had the ability to help out their situation, but none cared to try and so I'd given up on them. Growing your own food was by no means easy in the current climate let alone dealing with what the fat cat billionaires had done to the world in their gift of GMO products and population control chemtrail dusting.

What plants that had managed to survive through the dry conditions and fluctuating cooler temperatures didn't really stand a chance when it came down to trying to survive the soil itself.

The soil had been destroyed, at least the upper fertile layers of it had been.

In a combination of GMO enzymes released into the ground by GMO plants and ingredients within the heavy metal laden chemtrails doled out heavily just before the disaster two years ago the result achieved had been the rendering of the upper soil levels becoming inert of any nutritional or biological value.

The soil literally wouldn't grow anything or anything half decent anyway.

The only solution that I had found was to dig down and harvest soil not affected by the aerial sprays and use it for vegetable propagation. It was hard work and few wished to do it, especially as there was no gas to fuel the machines that could easily accomplish it.

The majority of people preferred to just rely on the white vans to feed them, as if they had become addicted somehow to the concept of not doing anything that would be too hard on themselves. The reality of it though was that they had seemed less and less human to me the longer time went on.

Even now they stared at me beadily from wherever they hung about the town, as if they were rats concocting a master plan of domination. I didn't care about being popular and I could take care of myself with or without a gun and yet the downward spiral I was witnessing in the majority of the populace left me wondering just where it would all end.

I struck out of town not bothering to take any of the wide open roads presented to me. I knew my way and without a qualm I stepped into the dry brush of the once fertile land that had become a wilderness of sparsely located weeds.

Weeds seemed to be the only thing flourishing these days as at least they had some tolerances to the chemicals used to render the soil's nutrients unavailable for normal plant growth.

My pace was quick as it was always a concern to me when I left my place unattended for any length of time. I doubted anyone in town despite the allure of food would ever care to make the five-mile hike, seven miles by road, journey to my place, but still there was the off chance that they would.

That was why I always varied up when I came to town so they could never build a routine of my movements by which to anticipate my actions.

Two years in the Marines had taught me to be cautious about ever establishing a pattern. As a former sniper, I well knew the benefit of keeping an erratic schedule.

Being a Marine was one thing in my life though that I'd like to escape from and I had tried. I'd come to this remote area and bought my farm and for five years things had been blissful and I had found a peace of sorts, but now...... now my new found dream had been taken from me by circumstance and a global conspiracy of epic proportions.

Now more than ever my particular skill set of once being a warrior seemed to come to the forefront. I hated it, but at least it served me some good.

Like right now!

I ducked and the arrow shot from a makeshift looking crossbow skipped on by me to slam into some brush. I rolled away athletically and sprang up to my feet to run a short distance before diving into more cover.

I kept moving and within seconds I was in a hidden, undisclosed position out of the direct gaze of where my hunters had been located.

Patiently, I waited.

Minutes stretched by and I felt the palm of my hand holding a five inch double bladed boot knife get sweaty. Then in the distance came a cranky sounding voice, "Oh come on Zeke. That wasn't no towel head anyways."

"So what. He might've had something on him that we could use for trade."

"The only trade item we need is some more towel heads. Now come on! I'm starting to not like the smell of these scalps so much. Besides that they're making me hungry."

Both men laughed together and I stole out of my position and crept to a ridge that gave me an overview of the two men walking away across the wilderness. They were scalp hunters, paid killers for the government, such as it was.

Their sole job was to travel through the outer areas and look for the fall guys that had been blamed for the decimation of the cities in the East. The rumor went that when the asteroids had wiped out the West Coast along with other parts of the world that Middle Eastern jihadists had seen their chance and had taken it in the societal upheaval that had followed the disaster.

They had set off dirty bombs all along the east coast and millions had died and millions more when one bomb had gone off as an EMP and taken down the electric grid for good. Ever since then every survivor of what was left of the country had taken it upon themselves to eradicate every last Muslim looking person that they came across as some sort of honor bound civic duty to those who had been lost.

The zeal was such in fact that one stood to gain profit by the killing of them and subsequently face scalping had become a highly profitable commodity if one could prove to the authorities that the face was Middle Eastern and hence likely Muslim.

How far America had fallen in but two short years.

Right now I'd rather be anywhere else in the world than this former entitlement society brought to grips with stark reality. Getting out of the country now though was a complete loss.

The East was unrecognizable and you'd grow a third ear before clearing the radiation along the coastline from all accounts.

This was assuming that all the reports one heard were true.

Who really knew for sure. As it was I knew of no one who had actually come from the East to verify all of the gossip of the FEMA personnel that had been passed along as if it was the gospel truth.

In general, I trusted FEMA as about as far as I would trust a snake with a sour disposition.

Once more, the urge to strike out and find something better than the decaying reality I faced daily, hit hard. The question remained though of who would feed the children in town?

My consciousness wouldn't condone the thought of having them turn into the bigoted zombies that the rest of the town seemed hell-bent on becoming. The urge to go after the two men and kill them was overwhelming, but it would be murder, and above all else I wished to leave killing behind me.

I pulled back from view of them and headed back on my way to my homestead. About an hour later I saw the buzzards.

They of all the bird species seemed to be flourishing the most. I knew what their presence signaled and I wished to avoid the death I knew I would find beneath their drifting spirals, but my feet took me that way anyway.

Some things no matter how terrible, just had to be seen. It took me twenty minutes to come upon the four bodies in the sand.

Their faces were scalped clean away, but it was obvious by other visible trait markers to see that this family of four on the run had been of the locality of origin that had been branded with universal hatred by all remaining Americans for extermination.

Looking now though on the bodies left to rot faceless in the sun all I felt was shame.

What right did humanity have to exist when we perpetrated horrors like this upon each other?

Americans felt they were justified to murder an entire people group based on the hearsay of others as to what they had done, but the timed event of over twenty dirty bombs going off at the same time along the eastern seaboard was a hard nut to crack for anyone let alone terrorist cells hampered by a surveillance state the likes of which the NSA was capable of producing.

No, I tended to think otherwise, but I kept my objections to myself and unsaid, as the message of the day seemed to be one of hate.

People were out of love for one another and yet needing a powerful emotion by which to feed off of they had latched onto hate as something out of the ordinary and Muslims fit the bill nicely by which to enact it upon.

The hundreds of thousands of Middle Eastern refugees that had been imported just before the world chaos had ensued were meeting grisly fates like this every day.

There was little I could do for the bodies as I had no tools with me and the ground here was too hard to dig by hand.

Taking my hat off I said, "God, nobody deserves to die like this. I feel bad for these folks, but I guess what makes me feel bad the most is that, well, I guess, because I know they're not with You. That would make things better knowing if that was the case, but....... I pray that You'd have mercy on them anyway."

I put my hat back on my head and looked away as the bleakness of reality settled upon me hard once more. What was the purpose in trying to survive this apocalypse that had taken love out of the hearts of mankind?

"Where have all the good guys gone to, God?" I breathed out softly.

"I'm looking at one." Came the quiet response from within my soul.

Shaken, I looked about, but I knew. I knew who had spoken to me and knowing that I had God's attention caused me to fret as to what to do all the harder.

I couldn't bury the bodies, but I could do more than leave them like this.

Feeling the weight of a Divine gaze upon me I set about dragging the bodies closer together. That done, I went about prying up rocks and laying them gently over top of the bodies.

It was hard work in the afternoon heat, but I labored on until a solid layer of rock stood between the dead and the buzzards.

Satisfied, I nodded to myself and turned to leave this forlorn scene of death, which is when I saw her.

How I had missed noticing her up till now I did not know other than the fact that her clothing blended in like camouflage with the sparse weeds growing about her.

Her eyes were what attracted my attention the most though.

They were directed fully upon me and they were all I could see of her face, as a traditional hijab covered the rest of it along with her head.

She'd gone to some effort to conceal herself and it had worked, as she yet had her face and life to attest of, but she wasn't going anywhere.

As my eyes took her in I found the evidence of an arrow shaft pierced through the calf of one of her legs. Then, with a collapse of energy her head fell back to gaze up at the sky as she breathed heavily for a moment.

That arrow had been reused who knew how many times to take down fellow kinsmen of hers let alone others like me, who just happened to be moving through.

I had no doubts at all as to the internal infection the girl must now have raging within her.

What to do?

I couldn't take her with me being what she was.

It didn't sit right to leave her here suffering either though.

About the only thing that did make sense was to finish what had been started and end her life as mercifully as I could and then bury her with the others.

My stomach turned sour and twisted into knots as I stood gazing at her heavy breathing form.

She seemed to be unconscious. It would be easy to do.

I could snap her neck quick and clean and it would be done and over with.

Raising a hand to my sweaty brow I took in how bad it was shaking. I let it fall and glancing at her lying there helpless I turned away as I had no will within me to do what needed done.

I made one step forward toward my homestead and stopped. It was as if an unmovable wall constructed of my own consciousness stood barring my way forward.

I gazed skyward for a long moment. Nothing made sense anymore.

Turning my head, I glanced back to see her looking at me again. Nothing made sense, but being somebody else other than myself made the least amount of sense of all.

Turning, as I was galvanized into an action that would likely cost me my life, I went over to where she lay. She'd pulled debris over herself as best as she could and I had to admit to a certain degree of respect for her.

She was a fighter. She deserved a chance.

"God help me for no one else will!" I breathed out as I leaned downward to start tossing the rocks and debris that she'd covered herself up with away.

Her eyes were very feverish, but interestingly with closer inspection, they seemed more slanted as an Asian persons would be. She was breathing heavy and in her one hand she gripped a rock but it went unused.

I slipped my hands beneath her and cradling her gently I lifted her up out of the shallow depression that she lay in.

She was a slight little thing for sure, but the prospect of making it the remaining two miles or so to my place was not a light task with her now in my arms. Still, I owed it to her to try.

Her eyes stared at me and watched my every move and walking forward I heard the rock in her hand fall to the ground. Like it or not, right now I was her only chance and she knew it.

I cradled her to me ever mindful of the arrow through her leg, but still it was made abundantly clear to me the pain that she was in by the softly expressed cries that issued forth past her tight pressed lips beneath her veil.

It was torture to hear her pain and I thought about snapping her neck all over again.

It would be more merciful by far to do that, but those eyes!

The way they bore into me kept me pressing forward as quickly as I could go towards my homestead.

The End of Chapter One Excerpt

*The rest of the story can be purchased at Amazon.com and other online eBook retailers **OR** you could check in with me via email and if you agree to leave an honest review a free review eBook copy of the book may be emailed to you.*

The choice is yours – in any regard I deeply appreciate the effort to support me in my work; however, it is given.

Sincerely,

Aedan